The Cowboy's Secret Past

Tina Radcliffe

LOVE INSPIRED

INSPIRATIONAL ROMANCE

LOVE INSPIRED®
INSPIRATIONAL ROMANCE

Recycling programs for this product may not exist in your area.

ISBN-13: 978-1-335-59724-3

The Cowboy's Secret Past

For questions and comments about the quality of this book, please contact us at CustomerService@Harlequin.com.

Love Inspired
22 Adelaide St. West, 41st Floor
Toronto, Ontario M5H 4E3, Canada
www.LoveInspired.com

Printed in U.S.A.

As far as the east is from the west, so far
hath he removed our transgressions from us.
—*Psalm* 103:12

A big thank-you to Craig Wolf with Oklahoma's Child Support Services for patiently answering all my questions. As a writer himself, he had particular insight, and I am grateful. All errors are my own.

Thank you to my team, The Wranglers, who have supported me for the last five years. You'll find many of their names sprinkled throughout the entire Lazy M Ranch series. A shout-out to Natalya, who named the canine star of this book, Patch.

Finally, this book is dedicated to reader and reviewer Susan Snodgrass, who supported Christian fiction and touched lives daily with her promotion of the genre.

Chapter One

"I'm eighty-two years old. I don't need a babysitter."

Trevor Morgan's grandfather shifted position in the wheelchair, jaw set, blue eyes determined. Despite recovering from hip-replacement surgery, the Morgan patriarch had dressed like he would have on any other day on the Lazy M Ranch. Gus Morgan rejected the sweatpants that the hospital physical therapist suggested and instead wore a plaid Western shirt, Wranglers and boots. The Stetson that sat on his thick, wavy, caramel-colored hair belied his mature age.

"Gramps, it's not a babysitter," Trevor said. "She's a registered nurse." He had repeated the same information nearly half a dozen times, yet Gramps refused to change his stance.

"Same difference," Gus huffed. He inched himself closer to the kitchen table and eyed the pastries cooling on the counter.

The drip and gurgle of the coffee maker was the only sound in the kitchen as Trevor took a calming breath. The aroma of fresh coffee mixed with the yeasty scent of cinnamon rolls called out to him. He would have liked nothing more than to answer by easing into a chair to enjoy a mugful of strong coffee and a pastry. But it was Monday morning, and the ranch came first. June in Oklahoma meant a list of chores piling up on the Morgan cattle ranch because the nurse scheduled for 9:00 a.m. was MIA.

"Gramps, this is not a debate," Trevor finally said. "The only reason your doctor didn't discharge you to the rehab facility in Elk City on Friday is because I gave my word that we'd have a home health team come to the ranch." He released a breath. "Besides, Bess is going on vacation to visit her grandbabies soon. We're going to need some assistance during the day."

Gus muttered under his breath and shook his head. "Define *soon*."

"Two weeks."

As if on cue, Bess Lowder, the family housekeeper and cook, walked into the kitchen with a basket full of towels to fold. She stopped, looked at Gus, and then at Trevor, her eyes round. "No nurse yet?"

"Nope." Gus glanced at his watch. "She was supposed to be here an hour ago."

Yeah, an hour ago, when his brothers Drew and Sam were here. They'd offered to postpone their vacation when it seemed clear that the nurse would be a no-show. Trevor refused to let that happen. The elder Morgan brothers and their families had planned a short trip to Branson, Missouri, months ago. A terrible plan, in his opinion. Though no one had asked him. Trevor's idea of a vacation was zero people, not a destination full of them.

His gaze moved to the refrigerator decorated with pictures of Drew and Sadie's children, along with the sonogram photo of Sam and Olivia's babies, due in December.

Seven years ago, a wedding picture of himself and Alyssa had been prominently displayed on that fridge. Bess had kindly removed it days after the funeral.

He pushed away the thought. Not going there. Not today.

"Did your brothers leave already?" Bess asked.

Trevor nodded. He'd practically shoved them out the door, assuring them that they could entrust not only the ranch, but also Gramps to him while they were gone. The ranch, he could manage. He'd been ranch manager for nearly two years now. But Gramps? Handling him was like trying to wrestle a greased pig.

And he hated being in the position of lecturing his grandfather. Gramps was the one who'd come to live with him and his siblings when their parents died twenty-two years ago. He was the rock they all depended on, who never once let down the four Morgan brothers.

So here he was, wearing a path on the kitchen floor, growing more and more annoyed and feeling guilty as the minutes ticked by and the nurse was nowhere to be found.

He paused when something caught his eye out the window. A small blue sedan kicked up the red Oklahoma dirt as it rounded the main drive and pulled up in front of the Morgan homestead.

A petite brunette in pink scrubs burst out of the vehicle. She carried what looked like a tackle box in one hand and slid a tote bag onto her shoulder. The woman said something to the passenger in the back seat of the car as she raced up the steps to the house.

Trevor tore out of the kitchen and down the hall, yanking open the door before the woman could knock. The action caught her off guard, and she nearly toppled over. He grabbed her arm as she swayed.

"I'm—"

"I know who you are," he said. "You're late."

Her hazel eyes were wide with surprise as she adjusted the pink stethoscope around her neck. Standing straight, she pushed bangs from her face and tucked a strand that had come loose from her ponytail behind her ear. She met his gaze without hesitation, the warmth in her eyes moving to sub-zero temperatures, which was fine with him. He wasn't here to make friends.

"My apologies," she murmured.

Trevor did an about-face. "Follow me." While his boots clomped on the oak floor, her white shoes squeaked an irregular beat as she trailed him down the hall to the kitchen.

All eyes were on the nurse the moment she stepped into the room. Bess offered a welcoming smile. His grandfather perked up with interest.

"Mr. Morgan?" the nurse asked, addressing Trevor's grandfather.

"Call me Gus. There are five Mr. Morgans on this ranch. It can be mighty confusing."

"Gus, then. I'm Hope Burke, your case manager." She grinned, the smile lighting up her face.

"I apologize for my delay," Hope continued on a somber note. "Unfortunately, I wasn't able to call. It won't happen again."

"Aw, no problem," Gus said with a shake of his head. "Not like I had a hot date or anything."

Trevor nearly fell over. One smile and Hope Burke had his grandfather wrapped around her pink stethoscope.

"This is my grandson Trevor," Gramps began. "I've got three other grandsons. Two are on a short vacation, and the other is in Reno for a rodeo." He turned his head toward Bess. "And this beautiful woman is Mrs. Lowder. She runs the place."

"Bess. You call me Bess, dear." The housekeeper chuckled. "Don't listen to Gus. He only flatters me when he wants cinnamon rolls."

His grandfather laughed. "I plead the Fifth on that."

"It's a pleasure to meet all of you," Hope said, her gaze moving between Gramps and Bess and avoiding Trevor.

Gus nodded toward the tackle box in Hope's hand. "Whatcha got in there? Are we going fishing?"

"Wouldn't that be nice?" Hope said with a wink. "Last summer, I caught a huge catfish over at Grand Lake. I'm ready to beat my record."

"Woo-ee." Gramps slapped the kitchen table with a hand. "A fellow angler. Glad to hear it. You be sure to sign up for the Homestead Pass Annual Fishing Derby. It's at the end of July. Cash prizes and lots of bragging rights."

"I will absolutely look into it." Hope patted the tackle box. "This is my supply kit. I'm on the road all day, so this is a convenient way to carry everything. My electronic notebook is in the tote bag."

"Looks like you're ready for anything," Gramps said.

She eyed Trevor dismissively and frowned. "Usually."

Points for the nurse. Trevor arched an eyebrow. She had spunk. He crossed his arms as the exchange continued, a bit intrigued by the woman.

"What's the plan?" Gramps asked.

"I'll be here twice a week. Each time I'll do a brief exam, including your vital signs and an examination of the incision. If your physician orders lab work, I'll handle that as well."

Gramps nodded.

"A home health aide will visit Monday through Friday mornings for about two hours. He'll help you with personal hygiene and assist with your home physical therapy."

"So I don't have to drive to Elk City for physical therapy?" His grandfather's expression was hopeful.

"You haven't been cleared to drive." Hope paused. "Someone will have to take you to PT three times a week." She smiled and once again looked at Gramps and Bess, ignoring Trevor. "Any questions?"

"Not so far," Gramps said. "How about you, Trev?"

"I'm good." Yeah, he was good until he could get Hope Burke alone and discuss the schedule. She was supposed to be here to help Gramps and make life easier for all of them. So far, that hadn't happened.

"All right, then, Mr. Morgan. Let's get you to your room, so I can do a quick exam."

Gus pointed to the left. "I'm staying in the guest room down the hall. Easier than the stairs."

"Perfect." Hope glanced around. "Where is your walker? DMEs are supposed to be delivered prior to discharge."

"DME?" Gramps asked.

"Durable medical equipment," Hope said.

"His DME is hiding in the closet." Trevor stared pointedly at his grandfather. "Gramps refuses to use the thing."

"Aw, well, I may have been a bit hasty last night," Gus mumbled.

Trevor nearly snorted aloud. A bit hasty? When Drew had suggested using the device, his grandfather had practically given a sermon on respecting your elders, complete with Bible verses to back him up.

"No problem," Hope said, her tone upbeat. "You've got a lot going on right now. I get that." She turned to Trevor. "Would you retrieve the walker, please?"

Sure, he could retrieve the thing. That didn't mean Gramps would actually use it.

When Trevor returned, Hope assessed the kitchen. "Your house is wheelchair-accessible. I noticed the ramp on the far side of your porch and these wide doorways."

"Uh-huh. Trevor's daddy did that to accommodate my late wife when we visited," Gramps said. "We've got safety rails in the restroom as well."

"That's great." Hope looked at Gus. "Ready?"

"I guess so." Gramps eyed the walker, his face screwed up with distaste.

Trevor crossed his arms and leaned against the kitchen counter, trying not to appear amused. Though he surely was.

Hope locked the wheels of Gramps's wheelchair and met his gaze. Her voice was low and comforting, and with words of assurance, she talked him through standing, pivoting and gripping the walker while she held the aluminum device steady.

Once again, Trevor found himself surprised. She expected compliance and got just that. Not unlike when he worked with horses. A firm but gentle confidence got the job done. More points for the nurse.

"Nice work," Hope said, rewarding Gramps with a megawatt smile. She looked over her shoulder at Trevor. "The wheelchair can go away."

"You sure about that?" Gramps asked.

"I am. Walking is the best remedy for that hip."

"If you say so."

"I do. Now, if you lead the way to your room, I'll do an exam, then we'll fill out a bit of paperwork."

"Okey dokey," Gramps said. He began a slow shuffle down the hall, with Hope a step behind.

Trevor stared, stunned. If he hadn't seen it, he wouldn't have believed that the woman had managed to get his grandfather to do what he'd unequivocally refused to do last night.

"Now, that was amazing," Bess said. She turned to Trevor and grinned. "Don't you think?"

"What I think is that this is never going to work," Trevor grumbled. The nurse's smile and perky cuteness worked this time, but eventually, Gramps would catch on.

"Oh, don't be so negative." Bess swatted his arm. "I like her. She's a bit of sunshine. We can certainly use some around here."

"Are you calling me negative?" He looked at Bess.

"Well, if the wet blanket fits…" A smile hovered on her lips.

"I'm not negative. I'm forthright."

"Forthright, hmm?" Bess leaned closer. "You're getting to be a cranky old man, Trevor Morgan, and you're only thirty-five years old."

Trevor remained silent. To defend himself would only provide proof that he was cranky. He wasn't. Not at all. He was simply a straight talker.

"No wedding rings. Did you notice?" Bess continued. "It'll be fun to see the wranglers around here stepping over themselves to meet a cute young lady."

"I didn't notice."

"You didn't notice which? Her ring finger or that she's cute?" Bess teased.

He jerked back at her words. "Neither."

Bess's laughter rang out. She held up her wrist and glanced from the silver watch to him, her eyebrows arched. "My, my. Fibbing before noon. That's a new record."

Bess had been around for a long time, and it was rare, if ever, that he could pull one over on her. Yeah, Hope Burke was cute, and yeah, he'd noticed she didn't wear a ring. That didn't mean he was interested. Trevor scowled and headed for the coffeepot. "Mind if I have a cinnamon roll?"

"Not at all. Have two. Maybe they'll sweeten you up."

He sucked in a sharp breath. Though the Morgan household leaned toward being heavily male, all it would take was Bess's alignment with another female to throw the dynamics into chaos. He sensed chaos on the horizon. Yep, they were going to have some real weather at the Morgan homestead, and he planned to find cover and steer clear.

Hope adjusted the tote bag on her shoulder. In one hand, she gripped the handle of her tackle box. In the other, she held a plastic container full of cinnamon rolls. Gus and Bess were certainly welcoming. For a little while, she almost forgot why she was in Homestead Pass instead of back home in Oklahoma City. She reminded herself to stay on task. Time was not on her side, and she couldn't risk being distracted from what she was here to do.

Unfortunately, her mission on the Lazy M Ranch involved the cranky cowboy she'd met this morning. She hadn't expected him to be quite so arresting. Trevor Morgan was tall and lean, with impossibly blue eyes and full lips that were wasted on his unsmiling mouth. There were shadows of sadness in the depth of his gaze, and more than once she found herself curious about his story.

It had only taken a few minutes to assess the Morgan household, and aside from the irritated cowboy, there weren't any red flags. As a home health nurse, she'd become adept at assessing family dynamics. Everything from mental-health issues to stress and undiagnosed physical problems. Part of her job also included evaluating a patient's home environment for potential hazards.

So far, the Morgans checked all the boxes, and she couldn't find a single outstanding issue besides what she was here to address—Gus Morgan's postoperative care.

An hour later, Hope completed the home visit without incident. The knot in her stomach eased a bit as she left the house. First visits were always stressful. Today, doubly so.

Hope scanned the ranch before her as she carefully moved down the front steps to the walkway lined with large terra-cotta pots of crimson geraniums. Overhead, a blue sky with wispy clouds framed the view. Green pastures stretched as far as she could see. To the right, there was a barn and a stable with a corral. The area buzzed with activity as men strode in and out of the buildings.

In the distance, the muted sound of a lawn mower filled the air. A warm, humid breeze brought with it the sweet scent of cut grass. The Lazy M Ranch was beautiful, and she couldn't deny a bit of envy at the wide-open spaces and large family that the Morgans most likely took for granted.

She'd spent her adult life in apartments in the city. Her patients had become her family, which was pathetic for a thirty-four-year-old woman to admit.

"Ms. Burke, I'd like to talk with you before you leave."

Hope halted at the sound of Trevor Morgan's voice.

She'd nearly made it to the car and far away from the disapproving glare of Gus Morgan's grandson.

"Yes, Mr. Morgan." She turned and put a smile on her face as he approached.

He wasn't smiling. Perhaps he'd forgotten how. The man was formidable. She'd give him that. Well over six feet, he was wearing a navy T-shirt that only emphasized his muscular forearms. The family resemblance was evident, although Gus had been blessed with charm and humor, which his grandson had failed to inherit.

"Ma'am, I have a ranch to run." He tipped back his straw Stetson with a finger and then crossed his arms, assessing her.

Hope tried not to stare while at the same time doing her own evaluation, taking in the caramel-brown hair that peeked from the edges of his hat and curled a bit on his neck. She didn't know any men who wore a five-o'clock shadow so well at ten in the morning. Rugged. That was the thought that came to mind.

She searched Trevor Morgan's features for a resemblance to the boy sitting in her car, but found none.

"I will work to respect that," she answered. At her response, she once again felt his penetrating gaze upon her.

"You look awfully young," he said. "How long have you been a nurse?"

Stunned by the remark, Hope worked to hide her annoyance. "I've been a registered nurse for eleven years, Mr. Morgan."

"Are you always an hour late?" he asked, his jaw tightening.

Hope relaxed at that question. This man had much to learn about life and the medical profession. It was her job to gently explain things to patients and their families. Even if this particular family member was being a rude lout.

"Patient care doesn't always align with minutes and hours, Mr. Morgan," she finally said. "Sometimes the Lord has different plans."

"Pardon me?" He cocked his head and looked at her, clearly confused.

"My morning appointment. He went to be with the Lord. That was my delay." Hope released a sad sigh. There was rejoicing at a soul going home, yes, but part of her job included comforting the loved ones left behind. The morning had left her emotionally fragile.

"Oh, I…" His face paled, and the deep blue eyes flashed with pain.

Hope immediately regretted sharing the information. Had she misjudged the man? Perhaps he was all bark.

"Then I left my phone in my car, and the battery drained," she admitted. "I'm not making excuses. Those are the facts, though, I assure you, Mr. Morgan. It will not happen again."

The cowboy nodded. "Um, you can call me Trevor. As my grandfather said, there are a handful of Mr. Morgans around here. I've got three brothers. Drew is the oldest, then Sam, then my twin brother, Lucas."

"I see." Hope stood awkwardly, not knowing what to say to his transformation from cranky to civil.

She certainly did not want to actually say his God-given name aloud. It seemed far too personal. "I'll be going, and I apologize for causing you an inconvenience."

"Yeah. Sure. Thanks for helping Gramps. We all appreciate it." Trevor paused. "My grandfather means more to me than…" He swallowed and looked at the ground. "He's important."

"He'll get my best care." As all her patients did.

The answer seemed to satisfy him, and he turned toward the house.

With his departure, Hope slid into the driver's seat of the car, turned to the back seat and handed her nephew, Cole, the cinnamon rolls. "Here you go. Your reward for waiting for me."

"These are for me?" He closed his book and peeked into the blue plastic container.

"All yours. You can save me a bite." She smiled. "You okay?"

"Yes, I sat on the porch for a bit, like you said I could." Cole ducked his head. "I'm really sorry I used up the battery on your phone playing video games."

"It's my fault too. I should have brought the charger cord." Hope shrugged. "Everything worked out. The Lord has us in the palm of His hand."

"What does that mean?" Cole asked. The eleven-year-old hadn't spent a lot of time in church, but Hope planned to change that.

"It means that as long as we listen to His still, small voice, we'll stay on the path intended for us." She smiled. "Understand?"

"I guess." Cole inclined his head toward where Trevor stood watching them on the porch. "Who's that?" He narrowed his eyes, his gaze intent as he stared out the mud-spattered windshield at the cowboy.

"Trevor Morgan. His grandfather is my patient."

"Does he own all this?"

Hope glanced at the view out Cole's window, where Angus cattle grazed in yet another pasture.

"I think his family does. Lazy M Ranch. *M* is for *Morgan*."

She assessed her nephew as she backed out of the

gravel drive and aimed the vehicle toward the exit. He was at that awkward boy-man stage. When he turned to her, soulful blue eyes searched hers. Hope would do anything to erase the deep sadness reflected in their depths. She'd been in his place when she was his age and had lost her mother. Only time and the Lord could heal his pain.

Her stepsister, Anna—Cole's mother—had fallen and gotten up more times than Hope could count, but despite her struggles, she'd loved her son unconditionally right up until her passing.

What about Trevor Morgan? Would he love Cole the same way when he found out the boy was his son? Hope blinked and swallowed back the tears that threatened. The ache in her chest seemed unbearable today, and she rubbed at the spot with her knuckles.

One step at a time.

Hope checked her rearview mirror as the tall cowboy faded into the distance.

The road into Homestead Pass was dotted with farmhouses and ranches—a pleasant drive into a very quaint town. Hope hadn't even known Homestead Pass existed until two weeks ago. She'd been going through the personal belongings that had been turned over to her after Anna's death. That was when she found a stack of newspaper clippings and Cole's birth certificate.

Cole Edward Burke. Her nephew's middle name came from Hope's father, who'd adopted Anna when he married Hope's mother. Though she'd given her son the family name, Anna listed Trevor Morgan as Cole's father. Her stepsister had never once mentioned Trevor, which was curious.

On the other hand, there wasn't anything about Anna that was not curious. She'd popped up at intervals in

Hope's life. Usually, when she needed money, a place to land or a favor. That favor usually meant leaving Cole with Hope for *a little while*.

Hope had found online articles similar to the clippings Anna had collected. A write-up that highlighted rodeo events. Some even had photos. Although the clippings were from different newspapers, they had a common thread.

Trevor Morgan.

Bulldogger. She'd had to look that one up. He wrestled steer. And he was good at it.

One particular photo showed Trevor smiling broadly. That smile was a secret weapon. No wonder he didn't use it often.

She'd done a little digging and come up with Homestead Pass as Trevor's hometown. All she had to do was pull in a few favors with a friend at the home health company. She got herself transferred to the Elk City office for the summer. It was providence that Gus Morgan needed assistance, or maybe divine intervention.

"Where are we going?" Cole asked, interrupting Hope's thoughts.

"To the inn for now. It's a nice place. Don't you think?" The accommodation at Homestead Pass Inn offered an immaculate one-bedroom suite, and Mrs. McAfee, the innkeeper, had gone out of her way to make them comfortable.

Hope had given Cole the bedroom and slept on the rollaway. The inn also provided a complimentary continental breakfast. Her bank account would suffer, paying for this and the rent on her apartment. And it wasn't like she had a nest egg any longer. That was long gone when Hope paid off the credit-card debt Anna had rung up. Giving her stepsister the card had been a huge mistake, but what else could she do? Cole was the one who suffered when Anna was broke.

She looked at her nephew. Cole hadn't answered the question, and she knew he couldn't. Because while the inn was far nicer than any place where he and his mother had lived, it wasn't home. Home was where Anna was, and that was no more.

"Will I ever go back to Tulsa?" Cole asked.

He deserved an answer, but she'd promised herself a month ago, when she'd picked him up from social services, that she wouldn't give him anything but the truth. And the truth depended on Trevor Morgan.

Cole turned to look at her, waiting patiently for a response.

"No. Not Tulsa." Never Tulsa. There was nothing in T town for either of them now that Anna was gone.

"Oklahoma City?" he persisted.

"That's where my apartment is, and for now, yes, that's home," Hope finally said. Eventually, they did have to return to OKC. But between now and then, she didn't know where the road would take them. One way or another, Hope had a list of decisions to make before she enrolled Cole in school at the end of summer. Where they would be at the end of summer remained the looming question.

Her nephew nodded slowly at her response, saying nothing more.

A profound sadness filled Hope at his response. Cole never argued or protested. Simply acquiesced. Eleven years old and far too accustomed to life happening to him without his permission. From now on, Hope would do everything in her power to change that.

Chapter Two

On Thursday morning, Trevor stood at the corral with one boot on the rough-hewn fence as Slim Jim, the ranch horse whisperer, worked with a mare that had arrived on Saturday.

"You going to that barn-dance thing, boss?" Jim asked. The tall, lanky cowboy pushed back his hat as he stood at the fence, waiting for an answer.

"I don't see a good reason to." Trevor did his best to avoid social gatherings and the dreaded small talk that always ended in nosy questions about his personal life.

"It's a fundraiser for the Homestead Pass Clinic. Food catered by Moretti's and there's a country-music band. That's a good reason."

"I can send a check," Trever said. He made a mental note to make it a big check. Dr. Lakhno at the clinic had done an excellent job of getting Drew and his wife, Sadie, through their first year of parenting Mae, their adoptive daughter who had a heart condition.

"Couldn't hurt to get out and socialize," Jim continued as he ran a gentle hand over the horse's flank. "You've been in a holding pattern for seven years."

Trevor leveled a gaze at his friend and the cowboy shrugged. "Just saying."

Not many people could get away with that kind of remark, but he'd known Jim a long time. The cowboy had attended Trevor's wedding.

At the sound of a vehicle approaching, Trevor turned and spotted Hope Burke's car coming up the drive.

If he hustled, he could stop and talk with her before she went into the house. Always good to check in with the caregiver. Especially since he might have been a little hard on the woman on Monday. This time he'd work on his knee-jerk responses and attempt to be more reflective before opening his mouth.

Trevor pulled off his gloves and shoved them in his back pocket as he started toward the drive. He did a double take when a furry streak raced past from behind, moving to the right, followed by Drew's dog, Cooper. Cooper, with his red coat and white patches, struggled to keep up with the energetic rescue pup the vet had dropped off yesterday. The rescue dog was part border collie, like Cooper, with the same pointed snout, except he wore patches of long, thick, espresso-colored fur, with a white face and belly. The pup had been in a fenced yard outside in the sunshine, but Cooper was a wily animal who'd no doubt unlatched the door and let his buddy out of jail.

"Cooper—here, boy. Cooper!" Trevor broke into a run, chasing the dogs so he could herd them toward the house.

Cooper's tongue lolled with abandoned joy at the game, his long legs working to keep up with his companion.

As Trevor got closer to the house, the back seat passenger door of Hope's vehicle opened, and a slight-framed boy of about ten or eleven got out and whistled to the dogs. Cooper shot straight for the kid, followed by the pup, and nearly knocked the boy to the ground. He recovered quickly and kneeled in the gravel, seemingly enjoying the attention of both animals.

"Hey, thanks. I appreciate the assistance," Trevor said when he caught up with the dogs.

The boy shoved shaggy brown hair away from his face and offered a faint smile as he rubbed Cooper behind his ears. "What're their names?"

"Cooper is the red one. We haven't named his friend with the chocolate patches. He's new to the ranch."

"Patch is a good name," the boy said.

"Yeah, it is," Trevor said. He nodded slowly. "Let's call him that." Though the boy's face remained expressionless, Trevor didn't miss the twinkle in the kid's blue eyes.

"You're pretty good with animals. You have a dog?"

The boy shook his head, a shadow passing over his eyes. "No. My mom… No."

Trevor noticed a book lying in the gravel next to the car and retrieved the paperback, examining the cover. "*Space Knights.* Love this series. Isn't this the one where the spaceship lands on Mars and finds a colony of broken robots?"

Cole nodded. "Uh-huh." He paused. "You've read this?"

Trevor crossed his arms and smiled. "I own the entire series. From book one and the discovery of the parallel galaxy, all the way to…" He chuckled. "I better not let any spoilers slip."

The boy's mouth formed a silent O of surprise.

Few people realized that Trevor was a bookworm and he took pains not to share that nugget. It worked out fine that he was often underestimated. *Cowboy jock* was the term given to him and his twin, Lucas, in high school. He'd surprised a few people, including Lucas, by graduating second in his class and scoring a full scholarship to Oklahoma State University.

"You're a big reader, huh?" Trevor asked. "Most kids your age are into video games."

"Last time I played video games," the boy mumbled, "I accidentally used up all the power on my aunt's phone."

"Ms. Burke is your aunt?" Well, this was new information. Her nephew had drained her phone battery on Monday, and she hadn't thrown the kid under the bus. He might need to rethink his initial evaluation of the woman.

The kid nodded and accepted the book from Trevor.

"I'm Trevor. What's your name?"

"Cole Burke."

"Nice to meet you, Cole." Trevor paused. "Do you wait in the car while she sees her patients?"

"Yeah, nothing else to do in the summer."

Trevor's jaw dropped at Cole's response. "Are you serious? There's nothing *but* stuff to do around here in the summer. Horseback riding for one. And swimming, and tubing in the creek. Then there's the Blueberry Festival and the Fourth of July parade, followed by a big fishing derby later in July. Lots to do."

"Yeah, but I don't live here."

"Where do you live?"

"I'm from Tulsa but…my mom died, so I'm staying with my aunt."

"I see," Trevor murmured. Though he sure didn't. Where was the kid's father? Sounded like a complicated story. Poor fella had lost his mother and was now stuck with his aunt for the summer when he ought to be out enjoying his youth.

Trevor recalled the summer his folks died. He'd been only a few years older than Cole. Lousiest summer on record. Yeah, he could absolutely relate to this kid.

"Would you like to look around the ranch?" The invitation jumped out of Trevor's mouth before he could think about the wisdom of the offer. Might not be a good idea to get tangled up in Hope Burke's business.

When Cole's head jerked up, and excitement lit up his eyes, Trevor knew it was too late to take back the offer. And maybe he really didn't want to.

Cole searched Trevor's face. "Really?"

"Sure. Ever been on a ranch?"

The boy shook his head. "Nope. But my mom used to ride horses in the rodeo before she had me."

"How about that." Trevor paused, his eyes on the house. "Wait right here. I'll run inside and ask your aunt if it's okay to show you around."

Trevor took the stairs two at a time. For some reason, the idea of showing this quiet, bookish city kid the ranch had a growing appeal. He'd mentored kids at the pastor's request in the past and always found the time fulfilling and enlightening for himself and his guest.

Maybe because the ranch meant so much to him. The Lazy M had provided a healing balm at the lowest points of his life. When he was hurting or confused, he'd ride far as he could and talk to the Lord. His Alcoholics Anonymous sponsor had told him numerous times how blessed he was to have a supportive family and all this space on the ranch to work out his thoughts.

He was right. Twelve years clean, and a day never went by that he didn't thank the good Lord for every blessing.

Trevor found Hope Burke and his grandfather seated at the kitchen table.

Gramps looked up. "Hey there, Trevor, what's up?"

"Just checking in," Trevor said. "And I had a question."

"Because your brothers calling twice a day might not be enough checking in?" Gramps asked with a chuckle.

"We love you, Gramps." Trevor's gaze skimmed the papers on the table. "What's going on?"

"Hope is doing a *postoperative cognitive evaluation.*" Gus looked at the brunette seated across from him, her back to Trevor. "Did I get that right?"

"Yes," Hope replied. She didn't turn to face him as she sorted the papers. "Your grandfather mentioned he had a few memory issues. I'm doing a quick evaluation, and then I'll report to his physician."

Heart pounding, Trevor gripped the kitchen counter. Memory issues? This was his grandfather. His rock. "Should we call a specialist?"

"There's nothing to be concerned about right now. It's not unusual for anesthesia from surgery to impair cognitive ability post-op. That's why it's so important for your grandfather to be mobile and exercise. I'll recommend some techniques to keep him sharp. You know, like word games and puzzles." She paused and looked at his grandfather. "He's very compliant. By far my best patient."

"You hear that?" A grin split Gus's face. "Her best patient."

"I don't doubt that." His grandfather appreciated the attention he was getting, and rightly so. He'd spent the last twenty-some years taking care of everyone else.

"What did you say you need, Trev?" Gramps asked.

Rattled by the conversation, Trevor nearly forgot why he was there. "I, um…" He paused. "I came in to ask Ms. Burke if she'd mind if I gave Cole a tour of the ranch."

Hope swiveled in her chair to look at him, her eyebrows knit with concern.

"Cole?" Gramps frowned. "Who's Cole?"

"My nephew," Hope said. "He reads in the car while I visit patients."

"That's got to be mighty boring," Gramps said.

"It's a temporary situation. I hope to have him in a summer program soon."

"Is that a yes?" Trevor asked. "I've got a thirty- or forty-minute window before I'm due at a meeting with one of my vendors."

Hope's lips thinned and she frowned. "Oh, I don't know. Cole is…vulnerable. He's had a rough time."

"Trevor sure can relate to that. Maybe that's why he's so good with kids," Gramps said. "Tell her about your project."

"I, um…" Trevor hesitated. He didn't like to talk about himself, though he had to admit his grandfather's assessment was spot on. Yeah, he liked kids. They didn't ask awkward questions about his wife or his past, or pry into his business.

"You earned bragging rights, son," Gramps said. "Trevor here started a kids event on the ranch last August. Right before school began," his grandfather continued. "Brought in kids from the city. The Homestead Pass Community Church sponsored the program." He smiled. "Doing it again, this summer. Right, Trev?"

"Yes, sir."

"Really?" Hope cocked her head and assessed him. "You like kids?"

Don't look so surprised. Trevor worked to keep his mouth shut, for Cole's sake, and simply nodded.

"I suppose it will be okay." She paused. "You aren't going to put him on a horse or anything, right?"

"No, ma'am. As I said, I have about forty minutes," he returned, frowning. What did the woman have against horses?

"Well, then, sure." Hope reached for her cell phone. "I should give you my number."

"Ms. Burke. He'll be fine." Trevor felt her gaze follow him long after he left the room.

"Did she say yes?" Cole asked when Trevor met him outside. The boy stood next to the pickup, eager-faced, in faded blue jeans a size too large and a once-white T-shirt with some sort of comic-book character on the front. He was stroking the velvet fur of the pup, newly named Patch.

"She sure did." Trevor smiled. "Come on. We'll put the dogs up and then get the ute."

"Ute?"

"A utility vehicle." Trevor pivoted on his boot heel and started toward the barn. He whistled for Cooper, who followed, with Patch bringing up the rear.

"How old are you?" Trevor asked Cole.

"Almost twelve." The kid scrambled along, his short legs moving like scissors as he worked to keep up the pace.

Trevor frowned and looked down at the boy at his side. "How almost is almost?"

The boy's face pinkened. The pinker he got, the more the sprinkling of freckles across his nose stood out. "In six months."

"Yep, that's almost twelve." Trevor swallowed a smile and tried to remember the best part of ranch life when he was Cole's age. Definitely the horses. "What do you want to see first?"

"Horses."

"Horses it is," Trevor said.

Once Cooper and Patch were put in the outdoor pen, with the latch firmly in place, Trevor cocked his head to the right. "The stables are right next to the barn."

The big doors were open, the fans moving the June air through the long building as they stepped inside.

"It smells kinda bad." Cole put his hand over his nose and mouth.

"Does it?" Trevor had long gotten over the many intense aromas on the ranch. All part of a day's work as ranch manager.

"What is it?" Cole asked.

"The smell? Manure." Trevor grinned. "You get used to it eventually."

His face pale and moist, Cole shook his head, contradicting Trevor's assertion.

Concern had Trevor putting a hand on Cole's elbow and leading him back outside. "On the other hand, maybe we should start you out slow. Let's go visit the corral, and you can see the horses in the fresh air."

Cole bent over and coughed once they were in the sunshine.

"There now. Take a deep breath."

"It really does smell bad," Cole said. He wiped his face with the tail of his T-shirt and darted a look at Trevor, his expression sheepish.

"You never had a pet?"

Cole shook his head.

"Cleaning up after an animal can be smelly," Trevor reassured him. "You get used to it." He nodded toward the wood fence. "You can sit up there and watch Slim Jim."

"You named the horse Slim Jim?" The boy's eyes widened.

"Not the horse. The cowboy. He's a horse trainer.

We recently started boarding and training horses on the ranch." Both Trevor and Cole were silent as the lean cowboy in the corral slowly approached the chestnut mare with a striped blanket over his shoulder.

"What's he doing with that blanket?" Cole asked. The boy stepped onto a fence rung, his untied sneaker laces trailing in the dirt.

"He's letting the horse sniff the saddle blanket. Now, watch."

Cole stared with interest as Jim gently touched the blanket to the horse's neck and then his withers, finally settling it on its back.

"Why's he doing that?" Cole asked.

"You have to take it slow. Jim is allowing the animal to become accustomed to the weight on his back. Eventually, he'll put a saddle on the horse, and when the animal is ready, he'll sit on him and let the horse get used to the idea."

The boy nodded, his attention never leaving the corral. For minutes, they were silent as Jim continued training.

"I'd like to ride a horse someday," Cole said. "I'm kinda scared of them now, but I could maybe start like Jim. Just sit on one." He looked at Trevor, his guileless blue eyes questioning.

Quirky kid. Almost twelve years old. If Alyssa was alive, they might have had a kid or two by now. The thought didn't hurt quite as much as it used to.

Trevor smiled at the earnest expression on Cole's face. Something about this particular kid tugged at Trevor, and he couldn't say no to the unspoken plea.

"If you're here for the summer, we can work up to that," Trevor said.

Delight flickered in the boy's eyes, and then he frowned

as though tamping down any premature expectations. "What does 'work up to that' mean?"

Trevor pointed a thumb toward the stables. "It means you have to get used to the stink because preparation to ride starts in there."

"Oh." Cole chewed his lip, thinking hard. "I can do that."

"You think so?"

"Yes, sir."

This kid had grit, and once again Trevor found himself longing to champion the boy. "Great." He offered a high five.

Cole looked at him for a moment before his palm shot up and met Trevor's.

"It's a deal then. All we have to do is get your aunt's permission." Trevor glanced around and then lowered his voice. "Leave that part to me."

Hope Burke wasn't going to be happy. She'd made it clear that she thought he wasn't qualified to keep an eye on her nephew. Trevor grinned. Was it bad that he looked forward to proving her wrong?

"And then he took me to see the cows. I mean cattle. There's a difference between cows and cattle, you know." Cole looked up at Hope as they strolled down Main Street. His brow was furrowed, his expression intent. "All cows are cattle, but not all cattle are cows."

"Yes. You said that." Hope's lips twitched at his serious tone. "I guess you had a good time yesterday."

Cole nodded. "We drove in a ute. That means utility vehicle."

"Right. You mentioned that earlier."

"I named the new dog too. Patch. That dog really likes me."

"That's nice." The sound of laces slapping against the sidewalk had Hope glancing down. "Cole, your sneakers are untied."

He kneeled down and tied them, then skipped a few steps to catch up with her.

Cole skipped. This was the happiest she'd ever seen him, except when his mother showed up after disappearing for days. Eventually, Anna would recall that she'd left her son at Hope's house. In she'd waltz, with presents and kisses, and everything would be forgiven.

A sigh slipped from Hope's lips at the unfairness of it all. Her nephew had no idea what consistency and security were. She suspected that he wasn't accustomed to any sort of routine. He'd spent most of his life as a mini adult to a sweet but chaotic mother.

Hope did her best to ground him in the security of routine while not stripping him of his past. Which explained why she hadn't insisted on new clothes and a haircut. Her goal for now was to prove she would never let him down and to retrieve his lost childhood. An overreach for sure. But she had to try. Cole deserved as much.

If someone had done that for her when her mother died, perhaps she would have grown up with fewer walls erected.

Ahead of them, a group of middle-aged women walking on the sidewalk approached. Carrying bright-colored shopping bags on their arms, they chattered and laughed, offering nods of greeting.

Hope smiled in return. When another group of shoppers passed, she grabbed Cole's elbow and pulled him out of the way. "Watch where you're going, sweetie."

The sidewalks of downtown Homestead Pass were certainly busy. Tourist season, she supposed.

"Trevor says that I'm really smart," Cole said.

"You are," Hope agreed.

She'd heard "Trevor says" at least a dozen times since yesterday's tour of the ranch. The grumpy cowboy had made more progress with Cole in thirty minutes than she had in a month. It had surprised her to learn that Trevor had a soft spot for children, but it worked in Hope's favor because now he had a son. And he needed to know the truth. Hope had lost more than a few hours of sleep when she'd recognized that she would be the one to break the news to him. It was time, and her stomach was in knots. She'd need to talk to him next week at the ranch.

"Right here," Hope said as she and Cole reached the local bookstore near the end of Main Street. The black awning said The Book Nook. She held open the door and let Cole step inside first.

"This looks like a fun place, doesn't it?" she asked quietly.

Cole nodded, his eyes fixed on the colorful posters and the tall rows of books.

Hope tucked a twenty-dollar bill into his palm. "I'm going over to the drugstore to pick up some things. Wait for me inside the bookstore, please."

"Is this all mine?" Cole stared at the bill in his hand, his mouth gaping with awe.

"Yes. All yours. Buy some books. It's going to be a long summer."

Again, he nodded, his gaze returning to the bookshelves.

"Did you hear what I said about waiting for me in the store?" When he didn't answer, she put a hand on his shoulder. "Cole, are you listening?"

"Don't worry. I'll keep an eye on him." A pretty,

middle-aged woman with silver-blond hair came around from behind the cash register. "I'm Eleanor Pickett. Oops. I mean Moretti." She laughed, her eyes twinkling with delight. "I'm a newlywed. Still getting used to my new last name."

"Congratulations," Hope said. "Nice to meet you. This is my nephew, Cole, and I'm Hope."

"Wonderful to meet you." Eleanor smiled. "Go ahead and run your errands. I'll be here if this young man has any questions."

"Thanks so much," Hope said. "I won't be longer than fifteen minutes."

"Oh, take your time. Have a cup of coffee at Brew's. It takes some time to find the right book. You don't want to rush him." Eleanor gave Hope a conspiratorial wink.

"Are you sure?" Hope knew she had to learn to give Cole a little freedom, even though she was terrified of the prospect.

"This is Homestead Pass. He'll be fine," Eleanor said. "And I won't let him out of my sight."

Hope pulled her business card from her purse and handed it to Eleanor. "My phone number is on this. Just in case."

Eleanor examined the card. "A nurse. How nice. Welcome to town."

"Thank you." Hope stepped outside and stood on the sidewalk for a moment, peeking into the window of the bookstore.

Eleanor Moretti was chatting with Cole as she guided him down an aisle of the store.

Hope sent up a prayer of thanks for the kind woman before turning and assessing the charming town. Overhead, a festive "Welcome to Homestead Pass" banner stretched across Main Street. Smaller pink-and-green flags hung at intervals outside the shops, while pots with red geraniums, pink petunias and trailing ivy, placed at intervals on the sidewalk, contributed to the town's welcoming appeal.

Taking Eleanor's advice, Hope turned left on Edison Avenue, waited for the light and crossed the street. Though Brew's Coffee Shop was three doors down, she already smelled fresh coffee and began to smile with anticipation at the luxury of a few moments of quiet time.

The shop was a surprise. It would fit in nicely in an urban neighborhood. Comfy-looking cushioned chairs surrounded a low black table. Black pleather booths lined the storefront window, and a few cozy tables filled the rest of the room. Overhead, exposed beams and industrial hanging lights gave the store the illusion of spaciousness.

"How can I help you?" a smiling young woman asked.

"I'd like a vanilla latte."

"Hot or iced?"

"Hot, please."

"Coming right up."

When she received her drink, Hope carried it to a booth tucked into the far corner of the shop. She pulled a wrinkled white envelope from her purse and glanced around to be certain of privacy before taking out the folded birth certificate, which she'd reviewed over and over again in the last thirty days. Why hadn't Anna mentioned Trevor Morgan if he was the father of her son? It didn't make any sense. Anna always refused to discuss Cole's father. Hope realized she should have pushed harder and maybe she wouldn't be in this mess.

There had always been a fine line that stood between herself and Anna. Hope knew if she crossed it, her stepsister might not return. At least if the door was open, she could help when Anna made yet another poor decision.

Hope massaged her forehead with her fingers. A headache threatened to take over, as it always did when she thought about the past.

At age ten, Hope hadn't even processed her mother's death when her father brought home little Anna and her bitter and jealous mother. He'd remarried without so much as a heads-up and moved his new family to the country because Anna wanted a horse.

So Hope was uprooted from her friends without a vote. She'd adjusted and even came to enjoy rural life and learned how to ride a horse.

Her father wasn't warm and fuzzy, but she had Anna, and Hope loved her little sis. Things were tolerable for a while. Around the time Anna became a teenager, the household began to fall apart. Hope could no longer pretend she had a happy home. When arguments became the norm—mostly about money and Anna's wild and reckless antics—her father simply didn't come home one night. While she'd never had the close relationship with her father that she had with her mother, Hope hadn't expected him to walk away without looking back. By then, she was eighteen and Anna was fifteen. Hope couldn't stick around, not even for Anna.

She'd failed her stepsister. She would not fail Cole.

"Mind if I join you?"

Hope blinked and nearly fell over at the sound of Trevor Morgan's voice. Heart hammering as though she'd been caught doing something illegal, she scrambled to shove the birth certificate back into the envelope and slip it into her purse.

"Sure," she said on a shaky breath. Hope met his

gaze and then glanced away, praying he hadn't noticed her hands trembling.

He wasn't wearing a Stetson today, further emphasizing how much he looked like Gus. Trevor's hair was also the color of caramel, and both had the same thick unruly waves.

No doubt about it, Trevor was very handsome, and she could see why Anna was attracted to him. Yes, it was a good thing that she was nothing like her stepsister. She had zero interest in rodeos, or cowboys, and even less interest in becoming a buckle bunny. And she definitely would never get involved with an emotionally unavailable man like this one. Handsome cowboy or not, Trevor Morgan was a complication she could do without.

He slid into the other side of the booth and placed a mug of coffee on the table. The once cozy spot now seemed far too intimate.

Tell him. Tell him now.

The words started as a chant in her mind.

She couldn't. No. No. No. She couldn't. What if he rejected Cole? Hope didn't think her nephew could handle another loss.

Cole was more than excited about the ranch and the dog he'd named. If she told him now, Trevor might call the home health agency and have her replaced. Then where would she be? Right now, everything was about Cole's future.

Her plan was unfolding nicely. It was best not to rock the boat yet. Maybe if Trevor got to know Cole, he'd come to love him as she did, and then he couldn't walk away. Hope knew only too well about walking away. She couldn't—wouldn't—let that happen to her nephew.

"Where's Cole?" he asked.

"In the bookstore." Hope studied a tiny fissure in the wood laminate tabletop. "Mrs. Moretti is keeping an eye on him." She glanced at her watch. "Maybe I should check on him."

"Mrs. Moretti is married to my sister-in-law's father. He's in good hands."

She gave a short nod at the information and tried to relax.

"You're not working today?" Trevor asked.

"I'm off on Friday and Sunday." Hope dared to look at him and immediately regretted the decision. She was probably the most transparent person on the planet. Could he tell she was hiding something? She feared her pale complexion was pinkening with the warmth of her deception as he met her gaze.

Trevor nodded slowly, as if mulling her answer. "We may have gotten off on the wrong foot this week."

She straightened at the words. "You mean when you asked me if I was qualified to take care of your grandfather?"

Trevor grimaced. "Yeah. That. I apologize. I've been known to bust out of the gate before my brain is engaged."

Hope bit back a sarcastic remark. Now was not the time to air grievances. She had to make nice with this man until she could figure out what to do next.

"Anyhow, I hope we can put that behind us."

"Yes, Mr. Morgan. I'm sure we can. We both have the same goal. Your grandfather's complete recovery."

"Absolutely right." He turned the mug in a circle and then studied her. "I'd like to talk to you about something."

"Oh?"

"I'd like to teach Cole to ride. Maybe one of the days that you're with Gramps at the house, and then a few

Sunday afternoons as well." He paused. "I'm thinking this Sunday to start."

Despite having learned to ride as a kid, horses brought back memories of Anna injuring herself on the circuit. "I don't know…"

Trevor looked at her. "Do you have an issue with horses?"

"No. It's not me I'm concerned about. I can ride." She twisted her hands in her lap. When she opened her mouth to speak again, Trevor held up a palm.

"Hold on a minute. Let me plead my case before you shut me down."

"Go ahead," she said.

"I like Cole. He's a sharp kid. He's also bored."

Hope frowned at the jab.

"Now don't get all worked up." Trevor ran a hand over his jaw as though hesitant to proceed. "I'm not condemning you. The situation is what it is."

Not a condemnation? On what planet? Hope lifted her own mug to her lips and took a sip.

"I know you don't think much of me, but I'm happy to provide references. Pastor McGuinness can vouch for my integrity." He paused. "I'll be sure he wears a helmet, and I can promise to treat him like he's my own."

At the words, Hope inhaled her coffee and began to cough.

"You okay?" Trevor rose and came around to pat her on the back.

This time it was Hope who raised a palm. "I'm fine," she squeaked.

"Whew. First time a woman choked on me." He chuckled. "Probably won't be the last."

She cleared her throat, noticing the patrons around them craning their necks to see what was going on.

Hope reached for her latte and took several sips. Then she looked at him. "I think that's an incredibly generous offer…" The words were a hoarse wheeze.

"But?" He arched a brow. "I hear a *but* on its way."

Again, she cleared her throat. "Cole's on the small size for his age and he's timid. I'm not certain he could handle a horse."

"Size has nothing to do with it. But you are correct. Confidence is what matters, and you can trust that he won't go anywhere near a horse until I've given him the training he needs."

He looked at her expectantly, his blue eyes clear and sincere. Like Cole's. In that moment, Hope knew that she had to agree.

"You've become a bit of a hero to him." She paused. "He's had a rough time of it, so I hope you won't let him down."

"No, ma'am. I'll never let that boy down."

"All right then, Mr. Morgan. I'm going to say yes."

"Trevor. The name is Trevor. And I appreciate that."

Hope nodded. The man had no idea how prophetic his words might prove to be.

Chapter Three

"What do you mean I can't watch?" Hope sputtered.

Uh-oh. Trevor stepped back when she removed her sunglasses and jammed her hands on her hips. Her hazel eyes were hot with annoyance.

Trevor glanced over to the area outside the stable doors where Cole stood, head down, kicking at the red dirt with his brand-new boots. Today he wore Wranglers and a navy T-shirt like Trevor's. He hadn't even mentioned proper gear on Friday, yet Hope had wasted no time outfitting the boy in essential clothing. Once again, he noted her devotion to her nephew.

"Mr. Morgan, I don't think you understand." The words were spoken in a low voice, for his ears only. "Except for the bookstore, Cole hasn't been out of my sight for the last thirty days. He's suffered a devastating loss. His mother died a month ago."

She stood on the gravel path between the house and the stables. And Trevor stood in her way. Sunday had delivered a beautiful afternoon, and the June sun beat down on them as he scrambled to defuse the situation. Hope glanced from Cole to him, her lips tight. He gave her credit. The woman cared about her nephew.

"I am sorry for your loss," he said. "But I do understand, as I've been where he is. I'm probably one of the few people who truly gets what he's going through."

Trevor took a breath. He didn't share often, and it was never easy. "My fraternal twin, Lucas, and I were thirteen when our parents were killed in a car accident. A truck driver fell asleep at the wheel."

Hope released a soft gasp and covered her mouth with her fingers. "Oh, that's terrible. I'm so sorry."

"Life isn't fair, is it?" he murmured.

"No. Not at all."

"Thank you for providing boots for Cole," Trevor said. "And for driving him here on a Sunday afternoon. However, I believe it would be best if he and I worked one-on-one. I don't want him to feel like he has to perform. Besides, as I mentioned Friday, it will be a few sessions before he actually rides a horse." Trevor gestured around the ranch. "He's got to get comfortable in the stables and around the animals. Riding isn't solely about getting in the saddle. It's about cleaning stalls, feeding and grooming the animals."

He paused. "Cole is very sensitive. I mean that in a good way. I'll want to pair him with an animal as intuitive as he is. That might take time as well."

"I see." She'd listened quietly, her face expressionless. Trevor couldn't gauge what was going on in her head. Friday, she'd deemed his offer to teach Cole to ride generous. It was clear she'd revised her opinion now that she'd heard about his rules.

Out of her scrubs today, she wore jeans, cowboy boots and a pretty peach-colored T-shirt. The color favored her fair skin, and the dark hair that touched her shoulders like a silk curtain. All facts that he shouldn't have noticed.

"That work for you?" he asked.

"What time should I pick him up?" The response was curt, but the steam had stopped rolling out of her ears.

"How about three hours from now."

"Fine. I don't agree with your process. However, I will respect it." She plunked her glasses back on her nose—a lightly freckled nose, like her nephew's.

"Aw, come on. I'm not holding Cole hostage. Think of it as time off for you. Maybe you can go shopping. Or chat with Pastor McGuinness about my character."

"I don't go shopping." She narrowed her gaze. "And I already checked with the good pastor this morning after service."

Of course, she had. He worked not to laugh. "And was his response to your satisfaction?"

"You'll be relieved to know that Pastor McGuinness thinks you qualify for citizen of the year."

Trevor's eyes widened at the words. "That might be an exaggeration."

"Not at all." Hope shrugged, looking perplexed. "Trust me. I was as surprised as you are."

"Are you guys done yet?" Cole called.

"Yeah. Be right there," Trevor hollered back. He turned back to Hope. "Three hours?"

"Fine." She dug in her purse and pulled out a card. "Do not hesitate to call me if Cole has any problems."

"Thank you for entrusting your nephew's care to me."

She didn't answer. Merely turned on her heel and left. Unspoken words hung in the air between them. *Don't blow it.*

Trevor had high hopes she'd mellow once she saw Cole gain confidence. He'd credited the good Lord, his grandfather and the ranch with saving him. Now, he'd return the favor.

As Hope drove off, another pickup pulled up to the house. It was his older brother Drew. He got out of the vehicle, went to the rear passenger door and lifted his three-year-old daughter, Mae, to the ground. At the same time, his wife, Sadie, slipped out of the truck and unbuckled their one-year-old son, Andrew. They were here to visit Gramps and give Bess an afternoon off.

That was a good thing. Since Gramps had come home from the hospital, Bess had been at the Morgan ranch for seven straight days. She'd willingly volunteered, but Trevor came by as often as possible to ease her load. Lucas had come off the rodeo circuit for Gramps's surgery, but had had to head out again for the upcoming busy season. Most of the load fell to Trevor, as he lived at the big house with his grandfather.

He had a house on the ranch—the one he'd built for his wife. Though, she'd never lived there. He and Lucas had for a time. But he'd moved in with Gramps and now the place sat empty.

They were going to have to find a solution soon, because Bess had already booked herself a plane ticket to visit her newest grandbaby. She would leave in one week and there was no way Trevor could manage the ranch and Gramps.

Drew and Sadie waved to Trevor before they headed into the house.

He offered a wave in return. His big brother had it all. A wife, a family and a life on Lazy M Ranch. It hadn't escaped Trevor, when he looked at the calendar this morning, that today was the seventh anniversary of his wife's death. Married just shy of six months, they hadn't even completed building their home on the property. Alyssa had collapsed at her parents' house. Aneurysm, the autopsy revealed.

The pain never went away. It simply changed from deep, hopeless mourning to an ache in the middle of his chest that rose to clog his throat when he dwelled too long on the past.

"You okay?"

He turned to find Cole at his side. Head cocked, the boy stared at him with concern in his blue eyes.

"I'm good." Trevor smiled. "Got something for you." He pulled a plastic bag from his back pocket. Inside were two neatly ironed and folded red bandannas. "Put one around your neck and the other in your pocket."

"Handkerchiefs?"

"Bandannas." Trevor shook one out and folded it into a triangle. Then he tied it around Cole's neck. "Pull it up when you go into the stables. It will help with the smell until you're acclimated."

Cole grinned. "I can do that."

"When you're on mucking duty, I'll give you a dust mask." He nodded toward the stables. "Now let's get to work. First order of business is a tour of the facility. Then you'll be scrubbing the stall water buckets."

To his credit, Cole didn't complain about the task. The horses were turned out for the day, making it easier for Cole to gather the buckets. An hour later, they were clean, and Trevor had Cole fill them with water. Together, they replaced the buckets.

"Nice job." Trevor handed a dry-erase marker to Cole. "Now you can mark the job complete on the board outside each stall."

"Yes, sir." Cole offered a crisp nod as he accepted the marker.

"Come on into my office when you're done." Trevor headed there and stood in the doorway for a moment, enjoying the cool air of the oscillating fan. He then pulled two bottles of apple juice from the refrigerator and grabbed a couple of granola bars from his desk drawer.

Cole entered a few minutes later. He pulled his bandanna from his nose and sank into a chair. A fine layer of red dust covered his clothes, and his hair, wet with sweat, had been pushed up from his forehead in spikes. To his credit, he was smiling.

"What's next, Mr. Trevor?"

"Break time." Trevor tossed Cole a juice and then a granola bar. "You're doing a great job, Cole."

"Thanks. It's fun. I like it. Maybe I can work on a ranch someday."

"I don't see why not."

They sat silently, enjoying the respite. Trevor had to admit that he liked having Cole around. The kid was smart, well-mannered and eager to learn.

"Were you arguing with Aunt Hope?" Cole asked moments later.

"Naw. We were exchanging opinions."

Trevor narrowed his gaze, trying to put together pieces of the puzzle that was Hope Burke and her nephew. "Do you and your aunt live close by?"

"Aunt Hope has an apartment in Oklahoma City, but we're staying at the inn. I lived with my mom until…" He sucked in a shaky breath.

"I'm sorry to hear about your mama." Poor kid was still mourning.

"She's in heaven now. That's a good thing." The words sounded rehearsed, and the shrug of Cole's thin shoulders didn't convince Trevor he believed what he said. The kid missed his mama, and it hurt. Hurt all over. Trevor didn't want to be the one to tell him that it would be a very long time before that feeling eased.

Trevor took a long pull of his apple juice and frowned. "So if your aunt has an apartment in Oklahoma City, what's she doing in Homestead Pass?"

Cole peeled back the wrapper on the granola bar and took a bite. He finished chewing and met his gaze. "She's looking for my father."

"Your father?" Trevor froze.

"Uh-huh. I heard her talking on the phone. She said that my father lives in Homestead Pass."

Everything around Trevor became very silent.

His father?

Someone in Homestead Pass was the father of this sweet kid?

A thousand scenarios raced through his mind. None comforting. Twelve years ago, Cole's mother was pregnant with her son. That was a time Trevor remembered little of. His best friend, Wishard Mason—a man as close to him as his own twin brother—had been trampled to death by a bull in the arena. The accident had been Trevor's fault. Not a day went by that he wasn't reminded of that.

Trevor shivered, then shoved a hand into his pocket and touched his sobriety chip. Sometimes just touching the plastic disk helped anchor him and remind him that he'd given all that to the Lord a long time ago and he had to stop taking it back again.

"Are you okay?" Cole asked, alarm in his voice. "Maybe I wasn't supposed to tell you that."

"Hmm?" Trevor realized he had crushed the empty juice bottle in his hand. "Naw, it's fine. I was just thinking."

This was the second time Cole had asked if he was okay. The kid spent more time concerned about those around him than seemed normal. Most kids his age were much more self-focused.

Trevor glanced at his watch. "Finish up. We've got just enough time to show you around the tack room and teach you about saddles before your aunt returns."

Forty-five minutes until Hope arrived. Trevor tossed his container in the trash can, then pulled up his phone and sent a quick message to Drew. He would need some assistance because he and Cole's aunt were going to talk.

The woman sure had fooled him, looking all sunshine and smiles. Hope Burke had an agenda, and Trevor prayed it didn't involve anyone on the Lazy M Ranch.

Hope couldn't shake an ominous feeling as she drove up the ranch drive three hours later.

Trevor was sittting on the porch of the Morgan homestead. Was he waiting for her? As her car crunched on the gravel in front of the house, he stepped down the stairs, slow and steady, like he had all the time in the world.

Panic edged its way around her heart as Hope looked around for her nephew. Where was Cole? She fumbled to grab the keys from the ignition and quickly jumped out of the vehicle. "Is Cole all right?"

"He's fine. My brother Drew took him to the west pasture with the dogs. They'll be back shortly." Trevor met her gaze. His was hard and intense, once again assessing. Why did it seem that the man was constantly sizing her up and finding her lacking?

He cocked his head toward the outbuildings. "I've got an office in the stables. We need to talk."

Hope shivered. This couldn't be good. "Do we?"

"Yeah."

Her nose tickled when she stepped into Trevor's world. She barely heard the neighs and snorts of horses in their stalls as she followed him down the stable aisle to his office. It was like the walk to the principal's office in elementary school.

They stopped at a glassed-in room that provided a view of the facility. The small space held a desk, file cabinet and two chairs. "Did Cole do something wrong?" she asked.

"Nope." He waved a hand toward one of the chairs before he sat down behind the desk and folded his hands on the surface. "Cole tells me you're in Homestead Pass to find his father. Is that why you're here?" His stare became hard. "Is his father on the ranch?"

Hope gripped the arms of the chair tightly. She hadn't done anything wrong. "I'm a home health nurse here for the summer. Your grandfather happens to be one of my patients."

"Yeah. That doesn't exactly answer my question. Who are Cole's parents?"

"His mother was Anna Burke." Hands shaking, Hope rummaged in her purse and pulled out her wallet. She extracted a faded photo of her stepsister on a horse and handed it to him. "Anna was a barrel racer at one time."

"Barrel racer," Trevor murmured. His expression as he examined the photo revealed only curiosity. He turned the picture over. "This date says this picture was taken more than fifteen years ago."

"Yes. That's correct."

Trevor rubbed a hand over his face. "I remember her from the circuit. Hung around more than she rode. Fact is she was broke most of the time. A time or two, I gave her money. Once for a bus ride home. Maybe a couple times for a meal. No strings attached."

When he met her gaze, Hope searched for indications that he wasn't being truthful but found none. His story sounded too familiar. Anna was always a day late and a dollar short.

"Okay, now maybe you can tell me who Cole's father is."

She closed her eyes for a moment and then opened them. "You."

Trevor jerked back, his jaw slack, face pale. "Whoa. That's a leap."

Once again, she dug in her purse. This time she pulled out the envelope with Cole's birth certificate. Hope stood and placed the neatly folded paper on the desk before sitting down again and clutching her bag to her tightly, praying she wouldn't throw up. She wasn't good with confrontation. She'd never be compared to Nurse Ratched. Hope Burke, RN, was more like Nurse Pushover.

Trevor unfolded the paper and stared at it for a long minute. "If she thought I was her son's father, why didn't she say something, oh, I don't know, twelve years ago? And why isn't Cole's name Morgan?"

Those were million-dollar questions. Ones she'd asked herself over and over.

"I have no idea," Hope said. "Perhaps she thought you'd deny her custody since she was a single mother with nothing, and you're a rich rancher."

"Rich?" Anger flashed in the man's eyes. "The Lazy M Ranch is not run by any rich ranchers. We're a family operation that puts in long, hard days to turn a profit in a good year."

For a moment, he sat very still and seemed to study her. "Were you hoping to gain something from my family or me?"

Hope inhaled sharply at his words. Did he just say what she thought he'd said? "I…" she sputtered, then paused, working to compose herself. "Are you insinuating that I'm here to extort you?"

Trevor raised a palm. "I'm trying to figure out why you didn't just tell me. Why all the sneaking around?"

"I wasn't sneaking around. After locating you online, I came here to figure out what sort of person you are."

"Didn't your internet sleuthing tell you that?"

She bit back her frustration. "It told me that you don't have much of a footprint. Just rodeo articles about you and the rest of your family. I didn't do an exhaustive investigation." She swallowed. "As such, I don't know much. Maybe you already have a family. Maybe you have a criminal record."

Or maybe, like her stepmother, he had no room in his heart for a child who'd just lost his mother.

"I don't." His jaw tightened and he stared at her. "To all of that."

"Look, there's no need to be angry. Put yourself in my shoes. I'll do anything to keep Cole from getting hurt again. I'm the only thing that stands between him and the world."

Silence stretched between them. Trevor pushed back his straw cowboy hat and studied the photo and the birth certificate on his desk. His expression gave away nothing. Finally, he took a deep breath and met her gaze. "So Anna passed a month ago."

"That's right. Driving while impaired. Fortunately, no one else was involved."

"Again, I'm sorry for your loss."

Hope nodded and looked at her lap. She loved Anna despite the many nights she'd found herself on her knees praying for her stepsister, fearing things would not end well.

"Cole isn't aware of the circumstances of her death.

I got a call from the Tulsa coroner and medical examiner's office and drove to Tulsa to claim her belongings." She pulled the faded envelope out and put it on the desk. "Anna had these clippings as well."

"So not only is Cole dealing with the death of his mother, but he's processing the fact that you're looking for his father." He released a breath. "That's a lot for a kid, isn't it?"

She grimaced, her stomach uneasy. "I wasn't aware that Cole knew what I was doing. But you're correct. It is a lot. More than any little boy should have to deal with."

Trevor nodded, then picked up each clipping and studied them. He gave a low whistle. "I don't get it. Where has your sister been all this time?"

"Stepsister. Her mother and my father were married for a time. In truth, before Cole was born, I hadn't seen her in a few years. Then she showed up nine months pregnant. She's been in and out of my life since. Usually dropping off Cole on her way to somewhere. Often a rodeo, though she hadn't ridden in years. So, no, I don't know exactly where she's been all this time."

"You didn't ask?"

"All I cared about was Cole." The question left her rethinking her decision, and she didn't like the unspoken accusation. "Look, I didn't push because I wanted the lines of communication to remain open, so she'd continue to drop him off with me. It was the only way to ensure I would be part of his life."

The words sounded lame to her own ears, but they were the truth. If she attempted to guide Anna, her stepsister complained she was judgmental, and Hope wouldn't see her or Cole again for months as penance.

Hope pinned him with a look. "You're his father. Where have you been all this time?"

A flash of anger came and went in Trevor's blue eyes. He leaned closer across the desk. Hope almost regretted asking. Almost.

"Now, just a minute here," he said, his voice low and husky. "I want to clarify a few things. First, twelve years ago, I was a young, stupid bulldogger on the circuit. I was a different man. I'm not making excuses, but I'm not ashamed to tell you like it is." He took a deep breath. "I am nothing but a sinner saved by grace. Again, that's not an excuse. It's a fact. If Cole is my son, I will do right by him."

The admission left Hope without words. Was Trevor Morgan as honest as he seemed?

He released a ragged breath and continued. "When were you planning to tell me?"

"I've already explained that. I've been the fallback person for my nephew. Whenever his mother took off, he was in my care." She met his gaze. "I wanted to find out what sort of person you were."

"What if I don't live up to your expectations? What are you planning to do? Run away with Cole?"

"I don't have a plan," Hope admitted. She'd planned for everything but this moment. Ridiculous excuse, and he wouldn't believe her if she told him that she'd been acting on an inner unction. A gut feeling that this was the path. One foot in front of the other. A walk in the dark and believing that the Lord had His hand on the situation.

Trevor leaned back in his chair and folded his arms. The stubborn man she'd met last week returned. "If Cole is my son, I think he should stay on the ranch."

Hope gave an adamant shake of her head. No. She

could never leave Cole. "I can't leave him here with you. You're a stranger."

"You said I'm his father."

Hope stood and gathered the papers on his desk, carefully folded them and put them back in the envelope. "Maybe."

"More than maybe, or you wouldn't have gone to the trouble of leaving your job and your home to come here for the summer. That was a bold move for a maybe."

He was right. It was a bold move, and remorse would keep her awake tonight. She should never have come here.

"I want Cole to stay on the ranch, at least until we figure things out," he pressed. "I'll need to contact my lawyer."

"I'm not leaving Cole with you." This was a battle Trevor Morgan would not win.

"Surely you realize that if I am his father, you'd be forced to leave him."

Hope licked her dry lips while her heart pounded an endless beat. *He's right.*

How did she get here? A slip of the tongue by her nephew and now the possibility of losing the only family she had left loomed. In the back of her mind, she thought she'd find his father, and they would agree on a plan to keep Hope in Cole's life. Was she fooling herself?

"You're thinking with your heart and not your head," Trevor said quietly. "Paternity claims aside, I like Cole, and he deserves more than the summer you've offered him."

Once again, Hope sucked in a breath. "You don't know me at all, Mr. Morgan. All this…" She waved an arm. "All this 'sneaking around,' as you call it, has been for Cole, because I want him to have a better future. I love Cole."

Trevor lifted a hand. "I'm not maligning your character. Just trying to figure things out, like you are."

Hope eased back into the seat as her heart pounded, regretting that she'd come to Homestead Pass.

"You can stay on the Lazy M too." Trevor's voice had gentled, and he looked at her as if he understood the war waging inside.

"No. I can't. I'm your grandfather's home health nurse."

Trevor shrugged. "Quit."

"I can't quit. I have bills to pay." The tenuous line she was walking with her finances was enough to keep her awake at night. "Besides, the agency doesn't look kindly on nurses who walk off the job. They might blackball me."

"We could hire you as a private duty nurse, through the agency, to work nine to five, five days a week with Gramps. Take him to physical therapy three days a week. That would relieve my brothers and I from leaving our jobs in the middle of the day." He paused. "And Bess is about to take some time off, and I can't have an eighty-two-year-old man recovering from hip surgery alone at the house all day." Trevor shrugged again. "We genuinely could use your assistance."

"Private duty nursing is expensive."

"We aren't rich—" He gave her a pointed look though his eyes seemed amused. "But my grandfather saved my life once. I'm more than happy to do what I can to ease his, and I know my brothers would agree in a heartbeat." He fiddled with a pen on the desk, brow now furrowed in thought.

"I've got a house on the ranch," he continued. "It's empty. You and Cole can stay there."

Hope frowned. "Why do you have an empty house?"

"My plans changed. Now the house is empty. You can even take that pup Cole is fond of with you."

"Oh no." She shook her head. "I don't think it's wise for Cole to get attached to a dog, especially since I don't have any idea what the future holds or if there's room in that future for a pet."

"Cole is hurting, and a dog can fill that empty spot he's got in his heart."

Hope opened her mouth to speak and found herself without words. All the while, Trevor stared at her expectantly.

"What about Cole?" she asked. "What will he do all day? You have a ranch to run."

"No reason why he couldn't be with me during the day."

"You'd want him tagging along?" Was he really offering that?

"He's not a baby. I was doing ranch chores at his age. Cole can learn a lot, and I enjoy his company."

She couldn't help but stare at Trevor. So many thoughts were running through her mind. This was an answer to a prayer financially, and it would give her time to deal with the whole paternity issue. Still, it was a huge leap of faith.

"I'm going to need some time to think about this," she said slowly. "Everything is moving so quickly."

That was an understatement. Trevor had not only turned the tables on her, but he had also pulled the rug out from under her. Sure, she'd planned to tell him soon, but she thought she'd have a bit more time—the weekend, at least—to figure this out.

"What was the pace you expected when I found out?" he asked.

"I keep telling you. I didn't expect anything. I wanted to do what was best for Cole. It seemed I at least owed it to him to find out if you were his father since you were only a few hours away. I decided to see if you were the kind of man who would appreciate what a great kid Cole is before I took further action."

"Look, I've only spent a few hours with him, but already it's clear that, yes, he is a great kid who deserves a break."

"I'll agree to this arrangement…" She met his gaze as a worrisome thought crept in. "But only if you promise not to tell him that you're his father. For now."

He seemed exasperated for a moment. "Make up your mind. Am I his father? Or not?"

She stared at Trevor. The man certainly knew how to push her buttons. "Do you think any of this has been easy? All I'm asking is that we not talk to Cole yet."

"What about my family?" he asked. "I won't lie to them."

"I'm not asking you to. I'm asking you to avoid offering information until we figure things out."

"Figure things out." He nodded slowly. "The Lord brought both of you here for a reason. I guess we're about to find out why."

Hope's heart was heavy as she realized that, once again, he was absolutely correct. She prayed she hadn't made the biggest mistake of her life coming to Homestead Pass.

Chapter Four

The chair creaked when Trevor eased back into the soft leather, aged from seasons of use. The office used to be Drew's, and before that, it was his father's. Now it was his.

While he had a small office in the stable, this was where he could work surrounded by the comforting memories of the past. A photo of his parents, which included all four of the Morgan siblings, sat on the big cherrywood desk, just as it had when his father was alive.

Some days he felt ill-equipped to be the manager of the Lazy M Ranch. Today was one of those days. His brothers believed in him, so he'd do his best to believe in himself.

Trevor swiveled around and sighed as he stared out the bay window that provided an unobstructed view of Bess's garden and the pasture all the way to the horizon. He had so much to be grateful for. Yet, as always, it seemed that something was missing from his life.

He glanced at the oak mantel clock ticking away the hours on the bookshelf, his thoughts drifting to the events of earlier today. He'd invited Hope and Cole to stay in his house for the summer. Why? Because… well, because he'd been dumbstruck at the facts she'd presented to him. And in a very short time, he'd found himself very fond of her nephew.

Was he Cole's father? Could he even be worthy of such a title? Shame mixed with confusion as Trevor wrestled with the question.

A question that he couldn't deny with certainty. Twelve years ago, life had been dark and cloaked in despair after the death of his buddy, Wishard. He should have been in the arena that night. Chunks of time were missing after Wish's death, leaving Trevor ashamed of himself. One thing he did recall was the night his grandfather drove to the Okmulgee rodeo and brought him home. Gus and the good Lord had saved him. Gotten him dried out and put him in AA. Turned his life around.

"You coming to dinner?"

His ears perked at the sound of Drew's voice in the kitchen.

"On my way," Trevor called. He eased up from the chair and picked up the family photo, running a thumb over the surface. What would his father have done if faced with today's dilemma? Trevor liked to think he'd have done the same thing.

"I'll make things right, Dad," he murmured.

The aroma of something delicious greeted him as he walked down the hall. Savory and buttery with a hint of garlic. Was that roast turkey? And it wasn't even Thanksgiving.

Trevor stood in the kitchen doorway for a moment as the Morgan Family 2.0 laughed and jockeyed for seats at the oak table. Just a few years ago, there were only the Morgan brothers and Gramps around this same table.

It was difficult not to be a little envious. Drew and Sam had found happiness, and it showed on their faces. Trevor longed for what they had, but at the same time, he was hesitant to go after it. He'd finally made peace with the journey that had gotten him to today, and life was pretty good. Why go looking for trouble?

"We need to discuss how we're going to handle Bess's vacation," Sam said when he spotted Trevor. The number-two Morgan son pulled two trays of ramekins from the oven and placed them on the counter.

"Can we eat first?" Drew asked. "I'm starving. All I've had today is baby oatmeal."

"Daddy, silly!" Three-year-old Mae laughed, her blond curls dancing around her head as she moved. Drew buckled his daughter into a high chair that matched the one on his other side, which held one-year-old baby Andrew. Trevor's brother juggled both babies effortlessly before sliding into a chair between them.

"How can I help?" Trevor asked, with a nod to Olivia, Sam's wife.

"We're set." She placed a large tossed salad on the table while Drew's wife, Sadie, handed Trevor an overflowing basket of garlic bread.

"Good to see you, Trevor," she said.

"You too." Sadie held a special spot in Trevor's heart, as this particular sister-in-law had triumphed over a challenging childhood. Another reason Trevor felt driven to support kids in crisis with mentoring and the end-of-summer event he had launched.

"Something sure smells delicious. What's for dinner?" Trevor asked. He put the bread on the table and pulled out a chair beside his grandfather.

"Olivia Moretti Morgan's famous turkey potpies," Sam said. A note of pride and love was evident in his voice. Sam took a moment to plant a tender kiss on his wife's cheek.

"Enough with the mushy stuff," Gramps said. "Let's pray. I'm hungry."

Voices quieted and heads bowed as the Morgan patriarch led the family in prayer. Once "amen" sounded around the room, smiling faces popped up, and eager hands reached for serving dishes.

Sam nabbed a breadbasket away from Drew and chuckled. "Come to papa."

Drew rolled his eyes and ignored him. "About Bess's vacation."

"Bess and I have already figured out lunches for the ranch wranglers," Olivia said. "Everything is labeled and in the freezer." She looked at Trevor. "All you have to do is follow the instructions on the containers."

"I can do that. Sure appreciate you, Olivia." Trevor shook his head. The woman kept busy. She was pregnant with twins and ran Moretti's Farm-to-Table Bistro in town.

"When's Bess leave?" Gramps asked while focused on dipping his spoon into the golden crust of his potpie.

"Next weekend," Trevor said. "Her last day is Friday, and she'll be back beginning of August."

Sam glanced at the calendar on the fridge, and his eyes widened. "That's more than a month. I don't think we've ever gone that long without Bess. I'm sorry for Trev and Gramps. They'll be living on Trev's cooking in the evenings."

"Hey, I can cook," Trevor protested.

"Says who?" Sam laughed.

Trevor turned to his grandfather. "Tell him, Gramps."

"Yep," Gus said with a nod. "The Homestead Pass

Volunteer Fire Department agreed when they arrived. Best burnt ends ever."

"That's not funny," Trevor said.

Even Drew chuckled. "It is a little," he murmured.

"It wasn't a fire. It was smoke." Trevor groaned. "Mrs. Pettersen saw the smoke and called the fire department."

"Gentlemen, could we focus on Bess?" Sadie asked gently, while scanning the table.

"You're right, sweetheart," Drew said. "Bess hasn't had a real vacation in years. She has a grandbaby coming, so she's flying to Texas."

"Texas?" Sam jerked back, his face screwed up like he'd bitten into a lime. "Texas is no place for a vacation. Those Longhorns think they're going to whup the Sooners. Not this year."

Drew laughed. "She's not pledging allegiance to Longhorn football. Just visiting her youngest son and his wife."

"So you say." Sam pointed toward the end of the table with his fork. "What about Gramps?"

Startled, Gus looked up from his meal. "What about me?"

"You're only a week post-op," Sam continued. "You'll need someone here during the day in case you need assistance."

"I've got it covered," Trevor said. "I made an executive decision."

All eyes turned toward him, and Trevor met them all, determined not to back down.

"Good for you. You're the boss now. That's your privilege," Drew said.

"Thanks. But you haven't even heard my decision."

"Doesn't matter," Sam chimed in. "You're doing a

great job managing the ranch. We should have put you there years ago."

"Hear! Hear!" Drew said.

Trevor tucked away the praise for later, silently honored at the words from his big brothers, whom he'd idolized. He prayed they were right. He adjusted the napkin on his lap and sat straighter. "I've convinced Hope Burke to come on board as a private duty nurse."

"What's that mean?" Gramps asked.

"It means she'll be here nine to five Monday through Friday instead of two days a week. She'll be here while Bess is gone or until Gramps is released by the doctor. Whichever comes first."

"That's brilliant, Trev," Drew said.

Gramps grabbed tongs from the salad bowl and added salad to his plate. "What's she gonna do all day?"

"Get you back into the swing of things," Trevor said.

"Like fishing?" His grandfather perked, a grin sliding onto his face.

"Possibly," Trevor said. "Oh, and she's moving into my house with her nephew."

Silverware clattered, followed by an awkward silence that hung over the table.

"You sure you want to do that, son?" Gramps murmured.

"It's a house, Gramps. And it's been seven years. I'm thinking maybe it's time for me to stop reading the same chapter over and over. Time to start a new one."

Trevor stared at his plate, becoming uncomfortable with the discussion as well as the silence. "Pass the salad," he said.

Gramps handed the large bowl to Trevor and leaned close. "Proud of you, son," he said quietly.

"Thanks, Gramps."

"Quit hogging the bread, Drew," Sam groused. He snatched the breadbasket back and out of the reach of his brother's long arms.

"Save room for dessert," Sadie said. "Bess taught me how to make her Texas sheet cake."

With that, the conversation started again. Trevor couldn't help but smile. He was fortunate to have such a caring family. They gave him space when he needed it and never pushed him.

A short time later, Sadie and Olivia cut the cake and began to pass out servings.

Trevor looked at his watch and then stood. "I have to get over to the house. Hope and Cole are moving in this evening, so she doesn't have to pay for another night at the Homestead Pass Inn."

"Nice way to get out of dishes." Sam arched a brow and shook his head.

"I'll take your turn next time," Trevor said. He slipped out of the kitchen toward the pantry and opened the large freezer. Bess kept frozen oatmeal cookies in the freezer. Trevor grabbed a package of those and a frozen lasagna as well.

He detoured to the barn and greeted Patch, who dozed on a blanket in his wire crate. The pup looked up, excited to have a visitor. The animal's tail trembled with anticipation as Trevor unlocked the door, and he shot out of the crate the second it creaked open. Eager for adventure, Patch followed Trevor to his truck, where he put the crate in the flatbed and opened the passenger door for the pup.

"Sit," Trevor said. Patch obeyed.

All the Morgan boys had houses on the ranch except Lucas. Drew's was farthest away, at the top of the ridge, near the creek. Sam's overlooked the east pasture. Trevor's was a fifteen-minute walk or a short drive away.

Five minutes later, he pulled the pickup in front of a two-story dwelling, half brick and half gray clapboard. The plan had been to add on as needed.

There was no need. Alyssa died before the Sheetrock went up.

Patch eagerly followed him up the steps to the wide porch. The minute the key was in the lock, the pup shoved his nose close, ready to investigate.

"Sit," Trevor said.

The dog sat and whined with fervor.

Once the door was open, he raced in. The echo of his nails clicking on the floor filled the house.

The furniture in the place was covered with sheets. If he'd thought about it, he could have come by earlier and dusted. Trevor walked through the area, inspecting, then stopped in the kitchen to put Bess's food in the fridge.

For a moment, he stared out the kitchen window at the view. Maple trees created a border at the back, and conifers lined the left and right. Seven years later and they were already tall and sturdy against the sky. The sun had begun a slow descent, though it wouldn't be dark for a few more hours.

This was a good house. However, it held no memories. Alyssa never lived here. They'd met at a wedding of friends. She was from outside Seattle, in town for the weekend. The weekend turned into two weeks, and soon after that, he proposed, then they'd gotten married in her parents' backyard in her hometown. The plan was to have another wedding in Homestead Pass. That never happened.

He often reflected on that time in his life. How quickly he'd fallen in love and proposed. Had he rushed because he was afraid Alyssa would change her mind if she knew the shameful secrets of his past? The question haunted him.

A knock on the door had Trevor turning. Hope stood on the porch. He made the mistake of opening the screen before securing the pup. Patch once again took off like he was fuel-injected, nearly knocking Hope over. She reached for the door frame while Trevor grabbed the box in her arms before she dropped it.

"Patch," Cole called with excitement from the car. "I'll get him."

"Thanks, Cole," Trevor called back. He turned to Hope. "You okay?"

"Fine," she said, looking somewhat dazed. "I didn't realize the dog would be here."

"He's crate-trained. Just put him in his crate after he does his thing outside tonight. You'll both get a good night's sleep that way." He nodded for her to come in. She did, and the scent of vanilla teased his senses as she passed.

"What will I feed him?" Hope frowned, her hazel eyes full of genuine concern. Trevor found himself wanting to rub away the wrinkle between her eyes. He shoved his hands in his pockets.

"I brought you everything you need," he said carefully. "This is Cole's responsibility. I'll have a chat with him before I leave."

"That would be appreciated." She released a breath. "I spend most of my time worrying that I'll harm Cole's psyche. I don't want to mess up a dog too."

"Don't overthink this."

Hope offered a brief laugh. "I'm sorry. We haven't known each other long. Overthinking is my middle name."

"Okay, then." He bit back a smile, realizing they had a lot in common. He'd messed up plenty in his life. Now he spent a significant amount of time overthinking as well.

Hope stepped farther into the entry and looked around. "Who lived in this house?"

"I did, with my brother Lucas for a time. Sam was alone in his house. Seemed like a waste of electricity, so we moved in with him." He walked around the open living room and removed sheets from the love seat and two chairs facing a stone fireplace. He tucked them under his arm, taking in the muted Southwest colors of the space.

"It's very nice," Hope said.

"Needs dusting."

"Dusting, I understand. Dogs are another story."

"Aunt Hope, do you want me to bring your suitcase in?" Cole called. Patch stood beside the boy on the walkway, his tongue lolling with joy.

"Yes, please," she replied.

Cole skipped back out of the house toward the car, with Patch trotting behind.

"That's a happy kid," Trevor observed.

"Yes. You may have been right about a few things."

"I am on occasion," he murmured. "Come on. I'll show you around."

Trevor opened doors and cupboards, explaining where things were located, until they ended up in the kitchen.

Hope glanced around at the appliances. "I've only ever dreamed of a stove like this. Convection, right?"

"Yeah. It has an air-fryer option and, go figure, it's called a smart oven."

"Wow."

Wow? He'd tossed a couple casseroles in the thing

when he lived in the house, but that was it. From the look on Hope's face, he should have given the appliance more attention.

"I take it you cook," he said.

"Yes, it's a bit of a hobby."

"Good to know." Trevor nodded. "There's a couple of things I should mention."

Hope frowned. "Oh? Is this the boot-drop portion of our tour?"

Surprised by her response, he crossed his arms and assessed the woman before him. "Funny, I took you for an optimist."

She chuckled nervously and pushed her dark hair behind her ears. "Yes. Normally, I'm an annoying optimist. This has hardly been a normal day."

"You can relax for now. I'm only sharing the schedule."

"The schedule." She gave a short nod. "Okay."

"Cole and I will start at about nine tomorrow."

"Is that when you begin your day?"

Trevor nearly laughed aloud at that. If only ranching was a nine-to-five job. "No, ma'am. I start at daylight and end at dusk. However, while Bess is gone, I'll be home by five."

"What about your grandfather? Does he manage the ranch too?"

"Gramps was an electrical engineer before he retired. He moved to Lazy M when our parents passed and became our guardian. Gramps dabbles in ranching. Does a bang-up job of being our social ambassador. For that, all the Morgan boys are grateful."

"So besides physical therapy three times a week, is there anything else on your grandfather's schedule I should know about?"

"I'll leave that between you and Gramps, but normally he likes a few hours in town, and he's got regular functions that he attends. Like I said, my grandfather is very social."

"I'll talk to him. There's no reason why he can't slowly return to his usual activities."

"That would be great." Trevor paused. "Bess's last day is Friday, and she'll give you the rundown on the household."

"What about meals?"

"I'll be sure Gramps has breakfast in the morning. We have a routine for lunch. Bess will explain the plan. As for dinner, I'll be home in time to get it on the table."

"Got it," she said quietly, as though thinking.

He eyed her, uncertain if things were all right. The woman was hard to read. Not that he had any real experience with women. Before Alyssa, well, he hadn't dated much. Lucas was the outgoing one. "Any other questions?" he finally asked.

"Oh, I'm sure I'll have a dozen. Tomorrow."

"I'll leave you then." Trevor held out the keys, and she took them. "There's a frozen lasagna in the fridge thawing, along with a bag of frozen oatmeal cookies. Courtesy of Bess and the Morgan pantry."

"That was very nice of you. Thanks." She looked at him for a moment. "We're still on the same page regarding…um, Cole. Right?"

"For now." He glanced at his watch. "I'm going to go and give him instructions on Patch. Then I'll be heading back to the house."

"Thank you, Mr. Morgan."

"Trevor."

"Trevor." She hesitated. "No matter how this turns out, your kindness to Cole is appreciated."

"I'm only paying it forward. Not a big deal."

"But it is," she said. "A very big deal. You've changed the course of Cole's life, and we haven't even taken a DNA test yet."

"That might be a bit of an exaggeration," he said. He didn't want anyone to think he was some kind of hero. Far from it. "Think of the Lazy M Ranch as a rest stop on the road to tomorrow."

"That's a poetic take on things," she said. "But I firmly believe that nothing occurs by happenstance, Mr. Morgan."

"Trevor. And I'll see you tomorrow." Turning, he walked out the door, mulling Hope's words. Could a few weeks on the ranch make a difference in the boy's life? He hoped so.

Hope rested her hands on her hips, catching her breath. *Wow, I'm out of shape.* An early Monday morning spent chasing Patch all over the yard behind the house had proved that. The energetic dog thought it was great fun to outsmart the humans. Hope had planned to walk to the main house, as it was only half a mile down the road. However, Patch changed those plans.

"I've got his leash on, Aunt Hope," Cole panted as he led the pup toward the car.

Hope laughed aloud. The dog had bested them both. She didn't feel so bad after seeing her nephew out of breath too.

"Wonderful. Why don't you sit in the back with Patch? Keep your hand on that collar. We cannot be late today."

"Yes, ma'am." Cole's gaze searched hers. "I'm real sorry he wouldn't come when I called."

"Sweetie, there's no need to apologize. We're both new to this dog game. Tomorrow we'll take him out with a leash." She smiled at the mischievous puppy, who cocked his head and looked at her with an expression that said, "I'm adorable. Let's play again." And he was adorable. He was also in serious need of obedience training.

Hope slid into the driver's seat and took a moment to collect herself. She ran her fingers through her bangs and checked her ponytail in the mirror.

Trevor Morgan was a contradiction she couldn't quite figure out. Never in a dozen years would she have expected him to offer the little house to them. And what a blessing it was. Though if it were her place, she'd paint the front door a cheery blue and add pink flower boxes with white petunias and crimson begonias spilling over the sides. Maybe a few hanging Boston ferns.

But it wasn't her house, so there was no point in dreaming. She put the key in the ignition and backed out of the gravel drive.

They pulled up to the main house at one minute after nine. Hopefully, Trevor wouldn't notice that she was tardy. No need to get him grumpy again.

"Look," Cole said. "The horses are out."

She turned, and he was right. At least a dozen horses grazed in a grassy field, enjoying the sunshine and sweet spring grass.

"They're beautiful." Hope grabbed her equipment. "We have to hurry, Cole."

Her knock on the front door elicited a holler of greeting and an invitation to come in.

"What about Patch?" Cole asked.

Hope groaned. "Have a seat on the porch. I'll figure out where Mr. Trevor is."

She peeked into the kitchen and found Gus at the

kitchen table reading a newspaper while Bess flipped pancakes in a skillet at the stove.

"Morning, Miss Hope," Gramps said. He glanced behind her. "I thought Trevor said you were bringing your nephew with you."

"Yes, sir. He's outside on the porch taking care of his new dog."

Bess chuckled, her gaze moving to Hope. "You've got your hands full with that pup."

"You don't know the half of it," Hope murmured.

A moment later, Trevor appeared in the kitchen doorway. "May I speak with you for a few minutes?" He tilted his head. "I've got an office down the hall."

"Sure." She searched his face for a clue as to what was going on. As usual, he gave away nothing. Had he noticed she was late? Was there a problem? Maybe he'd decided to rescind his offer.

"Where's Cole?" he asked.

"On the front porch with Patch." She frowned. "I should check on them."

"I can do that," Bess said. She turned down the flame under the skillet. "You go take care of your business."

She nodded. "Thank you, Mrs. Lowder."

Hope followed Trevor down the hall to a spacious office. He gestured toward a set of wing chairs. She eased into one, and he sat in the other.

"What's wrong?" she blurted.

"Nothing is wrong." Trevor clasped his hands together. "I called Child Support Services this morning."

"And?"

"They were very helpful. Provided more information than I probably need." He looked at her. "Bottom line is that I'd like you to call and open a child-support case to establish paternity."

"I considered doing that a few weeks ago, when I first saw your name on the birth certificate."

"And?"

"I decided to check you out first, and I figured it would be simpler to ask you to consent to lab work for testing. It's a lot quicker than all that government red tape."

"While it's possible that Cole is my son, I'm functioning on the likelihood that he's not."

That gave her pause. What was his rationale here? "That makes no sense," she finally said.

"It does to me. Whether he's my son or not doesn't change our plans."

Hope stared at him. Was he afraid of the results of a DNA test?

"Besides, the fella I talked to told me that if I'm not Cole's father, this route will assist you in getting benefits for Cole, like health insurance."

"What happens after I open a case?"

"You'll meet remotely with a caseworker. Once we're in the system, then we'll have DNA testing done."

Hope put a hand on her knee to stop the nervous tapping. Yes, she wanted to move forward with finding out if Trevor was Cole's father, but a part of her was terrified. Of what, she wasn't completely certain. Losing Cole? Or maybe it was the idea of change. She functioned best with well-defined parameters. "How long does testing through child support services take?" she finally asked.

"A few weeks, give or take."

She blinked, doing the math. "You're talking two months. School starts right before Labor Day."

"Yeah." He shrugged. "That's nine weeks away. You agreed that Cole could stay for the summer."

"No, I did not. And your grandfather isn't going to need a nurse for more than another four weeks."

He blinked. "I don't see the problem."

Hope stared at him. Was he being dense on purpose? "I can't stay without a job."

"Sure you can. But if that bothers you, then go back to the home health agency and leave Cole with me during the day. Let the boy have his summer."

"I—I…"

"Or how about if we take it one step at a time?"

"I don't usually function one step at a time." Which was not entirely the truth, as it seemed that ever since she'd started on this journey to find Cole's father, she'd been functioning that way, and she didn't like it one bit.

"Yeah, I noticed you've got control issues."

Her jaw nearly dropped. "Excuse me?"

"Nothing wrong with that. I'm sure it's a trait that's served you well in the past." His expression turned thoughtful. "But the thing is, this is all about Cole. Not about you or me."

"I'm aware of that. I've been aware of that for nearly twelve years."

"Great. Then we agree. One step at a time."

Hope opened her mouth and closed it. She was accustomed to being in charge, but Trevor Morgan seemed to challenge her at every turn. The galling part was that his arguments were difficult to refute.

He smiled. "Aw, come on. We can work together, you know."

Work together his way is what he means. She shook her head. "Fine. We do it your way for now." She paused. "Is there anything else?"

"Yeah. He needs a haircut. The kid can hardly see

with that hair in his face. I'll take him on Saturday when I go into town."

"I'm perfectly capable—"

Trevor raised a hand. "You've got to stop taking everything personally."

"Am I?" she shot back.

"Yeah. Cole is eleven. He doesn't need his auntie with him to visit the barber. I'm getting a haircut on Saturday. He can come with me. Good for him to have other influences in his life."

"You mean men."

"No. I mean 'other.' Gramps, Bess, Pastor McGuinness. His whole life has been you and his mother. Maybe he could learn something from others."

"Wait." She did a double take. "Are you calling me a helicopter aunt?"

"If the propeller fits."

Hope scoffed, unable to come up with a response but knowing he was right. Anna's wayfaring lifestyle hadn't helped Cole establish much of a support system.

Trevor stood. "This has been a good talk. I appreciate it."

Hope blinked. A good talk? He'd done all the talking and the decision-making. She followed Trevor back down the hall. Bess was alone in the kitchen loading the dishwasher.

"Hey, Bess. Where's Gramps?" Trevor asked.

"On the front porch. Eating second breakfast with Cole."

"Second breakfast?" Hope asked. "Like the hobbits?"

"No, like the ranchers," Trevor returned. "We don't have much of an appetite at four a.m., so we eat second breakfast around nine."

The screen door gently swooshed behind them as they went out to the front porch.

Gus and Cole were sitting at a wicker table eating pancakes. Patch was stretched out on the floor next to Cole's chair, obviously tired from his morning romp. When the Morgan patriarch leaned over to Cole, said something and chuckled, her nephew's face broke into a wide grin.

Hope's heart stuttered at the sight. Cole deserved more moments like this. Maybe a summer on the Lazy M Ranch wasn't such an outlandish idea.

"What are you two up to?" Trevor called as they walked toward the table.

"Nothing much. I was telling Cole here about the time you sat on that red anthill."

"An anthill?" Hope murmured, pinning him with her gaze. "And you wonder why I'm protective of my nephew."

"Hey, no need to look at me like that," Trevor said. "That was a long time ago, and to be fair, I didn't realize it was an anthill."

"Yep, you were about Cole's age." Gramps grinned, his blue eyes crinkling at the corners.

Trevor grinned back. "Cole is a lot smarter than me."

"Can't dispute them facts." Gus laughed.

Bess stepped outside, flipping a dish towel over her shoulder, and assessed the table. "All finished here?"

"Yes, ma'am," Cole said. He wiped his mouth with the cloth napkin on his lap. "Thank you. Best pancakes I've ever had."

"What a sweet boy you are," Bess said as she began collecting dishes.

"I'll help you with that," Hope said, stepping forward.

"Oh, you'll have plenty of opportunities while I'm

on vacation." Bess looked at Trevor. "What do you two have planned for today?"

"Cole and I have mucking class," Trevor said.

"Mucking class?" Cole repeated, his eyes widening. "You think I'm ready?"

"Sure you are. I've got a mask for you, just like I promised."

"Are you sure—" Hope began, looking from her nephew to Trevor.

The cowboy met her gaze. "I'm very sure."

She offered a tight nod and worked to tamp down her concern. How dangerous could mucking be? The horses were already out in the pasture.

"The boss man is going to muck stalls?" Gramp asked with a laugh.

"Yes, sir. No one on this ranch is too big to muck. After lunch I have a meeting. Cole will be with Jim to observe horse training for the afternoon."

Hope glanced at her watch. "We better head into Elk City, Gus. Physical therapy is at ten thirty."

"Yes, ma'am. I can see you run a tight ship like my grandson."

"Not quite that tight." Hope looked at Cole. "If you need me, have Mr. Trevor give me a call. For anything. Okay?"

"He'll be fine, Auntie." Trevor arched an eyebrow.

Heat warmed Hope's face. She opened her mouth and then closed it again, crossing her arms in exasperation.

This rancher knew how to push her buttons and she was determined not to allow him to best her. Not today, at least.

Chapter Five

"Are you sure you don't mind?" Bess asked. "I don't want to take advantage of you."

Hope smiled at the housekeeper. It had only been two weeks since she'd arrived on the Lazy M Ranch, yet it felt like she'd known the caring woman all her life.

"Bess, you've been wonderful showing me the ropes this week." She glanced around the spotless kitchen. "But it's Friday. Lunch is over. Gus is taking a nap. Dinner is in the refrigerator. There really isn't much left to do around here. Go run your errands and have a wonderful vacation."

Bess gave a little wiggle of her shoulders. "You're right. I'm going to do that." Then she paused. "Sadie and Liv know the routine. Give them a call if you have problems. All the numbers are in that notebook in the drawer. And promise me you won't let Trevor get to you. I know he can be a bit intimidating."

"Trevor? Oh, no, I won't. In my line of work, I deal with a range of personalities. I think of myself as Switzerland. I stay neutral at all times with my clients." Her eyes went to the refrigerator, where a sweet photo of Drew, Sadie and their children slid from the magnets to the floor. She picked it up and placed the picture next to several others of the Morgan brothers. All were represented, except Trevor.

"Bess, may I ask you a quick question?"

"Sure, honey."

"Why aren't there any photos of Trevor on the fridge?"

The older woman sighed. "There used to be. They were all of Trevor and Alyssa. When Alyssa passed, I tucked them away. It seemed every time he looked at them he got that woeful face."

"Alyssa?" A knot of dread tightened in Hope's stomach.

"His wife. We lost her about seven years ago. She was up in Seattle when it happened."

Trevor is a widower. How did she not see that in her internet searching? Hope's heart ached at the information. He'd found love and lost love. The next time she had a pity party for her own life, she'd remember this moment. Perhaps she was fortunate to have never fallen in love.

"Didn't he tell you?" Bess asked.

"We haven't really talked about much except Gus and Cole and Patch."

"And he's not that talkative anyhow. Is he?" Bess added.

"Not exactly." A sudden thought crossed Hope's mind, and she couldn't help but ask the question. "Am I living in their house?"

"Technically, yes. Though the house wasn't finished before we lost her." Bess patted Hope's arm. "Trevor must like you because he's never invited anyone else into that house, except his brothers."

Hope nodded absently. She doubted that Trevor liked her. Aside from his assessing looks, which she interpreted as her not measuring up, it was Cole who was the cowboy's focus.

"Anything else?" Bess's gaze swept the kitchen in a final check.

"There is one more thing. Would you mind if I used your oven?" Hope asked. It would only be proper to get the cook's permission before she infringed upon her territory.

Bess laughed at that and pointed toward the hallway. "The kitchen is yours. Consider me out that door."

"Thanks, Bess."

"No. Thank you, dear. I am relieved to know you'll be here in my absence."

Thirty minutes later, the scent of chocolate wafted through the room as the first batch of cookies baked. Hope turned on the oven light and peeked at them.

"What are you doing?"

She whirled around at the sound of Trevor's voice. The perpetual frown was on his face as he stared at her. With his straw Stetson perched on the back of his head, and a black T-shirt and Wranglers, the man was formidable as he filled the doorway. Hope wasn't accustomed to so much testosterone and took a step back.

"I'm making cookies. Secret recipe." A smile escaped at the admission. Baking and cooking brought back memories of her mother, who had invited Hope to experiment with recipes from an early age.

Trevor seemed annoyed at her cheerful response. But she refused to let him get her down. Especially since the cookies in the oven were some of her finest if she did say so herself. Double chocolate white chip. Her absolute favorite. Not an heirloom recipe, but a recipe perfected with love over the years.

He looked around the kitchen, his gaze returning to her.

"You're awfully grumpy," Hope said.

"I get that a lot." Then he strode to the kitchen sink, pulled the disinfectant wash from the lower cupboard and turned on the water. That was when she noticed a dusty, bloodstained gauze bandage on the palm of his right hand.

Hope's medical training kicked in, and she moved closer. "Did you cut yourself?"

"Cut it last week and I accidentally opened the wound again. I need to pick up a different pair of gloves."

"Isn't there a first-aid kit outside? You really should have one in the barn and the stables."

"We do. I didn't want anyone to make a big deal out of it." He stared pointedly at her. "That's why I came inside to wash up."

"Oh." Standing straight, she refused to allow him to browbeat her. This was her territory now. "Is your tetanus up-to-date?"

"It is."

"In case you forgot, I am a registered nurse. That means I'm qualified to assist you with that dressing change."

"I got it." He pulled out the trash can, then unwrapped the gauze and ran the cut under a stream of water.

"You're right-handed."

"So?"

"It won't be easy to clean the area, apply antiseptic and secure a dressing." He glanced over at her, and she returned the same pointed look.

"Okay, fine," he muttered.

"Have a seat at the table." Hope covered the kitchen table with a protective pad and placed her tackle box on the material. She laid out all her supplies, carefully opening packages to maintain a sterile field, then donned nitrile gloves. "Could you put your hand on the table, please?"

He complied. "Sorry for all the dust. Job hazard."

"Not a problem," Hope said.

Silence stretched as she assessed the cut.

Trevor pulled out his phone and checked messages with his free hand. "Have you heard from social services?" he asked.

"Just a confirmation email. I've reviewed the documentation online at least a dozen times, and my lay interpretation is that the caseworker should reach out anytime now. You'll be notified, and then you can file an appeal denying paternity. We'll be sent instructions for genetic testing at some point in that timeline."

"The cogs of bureaucracy move slowly." He nodded. "What are you going to tell Cole regarding testing?"

"I don't know." She carefully concentrated on cleansing the wound. "Someone recently suggested that I take things one step at a time."

Hope lifted her gaze and met his. She smiled sweetly.

"Touché," he murmured. His lips twitched, and the half-lidded eyes offered a look of respect at her comeback.

Hope dried his palm and applied antibiotic ointment, followed by a loose dressing. "All done. It's healing nicely, though it's unfortunate that it's in an area that gets so much use. You should definitely get some gloves that will protect the laceration."

"Got it, Doc. I'll be in town tomorrow for that haircut. We'll make a stop at the Hitching Post." He paused. "You know what? I think we'll take Gramps with us too."

"That's a great idea." She pulled off her gloves and began to roll up the pad containing all the used supplies. "It's only been a week, but I want to tell you that already I've seen a change in Cole. I mean, besides the fact that he practically falls asleep in his dinner and takes his shower without being told and is up to walk Patch at dawn."

Trevor nodded. "Ranching is good for him."

"Yes. Absolutely." Hope cocked her head. "How do you think he's doing?"

"He's a quick learner and he and the dog are good for each other."

"As you predicted." She hesitated. "I've been meaning to talk to you about that dog."

"That dog?" He raised a brow. "You don't like Patch?"

"Please. Who doesn't love Patch? He has a heart bigger than this ranch."

"Yeah, he does."

"However, while I've never had a dog of my own, I'm pretty certain they're supposed to be a little less independent than this one. He doesn't come when you call his name and wrangling him every morning is getting old. Aren't puppies supposed to have obedience training or something?"

Trevor stood and examined the dressing on his hand. "I'll ask Slim Jim to spend some time with Cole training Patch."

"He trains dogs too?"

"Yeah, Jim's the ranch animal whisperer. He's been known to get the chickens to follow his instructions."

She grinned. "That I'd like to see."

The oven timer interrupted the conversation, and Hope washed her hands before pulling the cookies out of the oven and sliding in another sheet of unbaked dough.

Trevor's brow rose. "I'm still having a hard time believing Bess gave you free rein over her kitchen."

"She's on vacation." Hope tried to ignore the spark of irritation rising up. *Switzerland. Switzerland.*

"Yeah, but I saw you cooking with her yesterday too. Didn't you help her make that pot roast for dinner?"

"Actually, it was my recipe. Bess has been distracted preparing for her trip, so I offered to make it before I left for the day." She narrowed her gaze. "Why do you sound so surprised? And why all questions?"

"It's been my experience that Bess doesn't let anyone in her kitchen unless she's instructing."

"Instructing?"

"Yeah. Sadie needed training, and Bess obliged. Other than that, she's fairly possessive about that new stove. Gave me a list of dos and don'ts before she left."

"Sure, I understand. It's a very nice stove." Hope assessed the black, stainless-steel-and-porcelain appliance with its shiny black glass oven door. "However, I don't know what to tell you. I asked if she minded if I used her stove and she was fine with it." She paused, unable to resist a little dramatic effect. "Maybe she likes me. Some people do."

"I guess," Trevor muttered. He looked around. "Where is Bess?"

"She took off early since everything was done here and was headed to Elk City to pick up a few more things for the grandbaby."

"More stuff for the grandbaby? Is she having triplets or something?"

"No, but it's her first grandbaby. Grandmother's nest, just like mothers-to-be." Hope pulled a plate from the cupboard and transferred the cookies from the cookie sheet.

Trevor wandered closer. "You know this from experience?"

"No, not from personal experience. I've spent much

of my career supporting families. I can tell you that the birth of a grandchild can be one of the most anticipated events of a grandparent's life, often surpassing the birth of their own children."

"What about you?"

"What about me?" She blinked at the question.

"You support other families. Ever think about a family of your own?"

Hope stared at him, her mouth dry. Two weeks and he'd said six words of a personal nature. Today, he decided to be chatty and ask a question straight out of Random City.

"I have Cole. I don't need anything else." Or any*one* else. As a young girl she hadn't seen beyond the loving bubble of care her mother provided. She hadn't recognized her father's coldness. When her mother passed, everything changed. That was when she learned not to need anyone. Life was much easier that way.

She glanced at the big clock on the wall, eager to change the subject. "Where is he, anyhow?"

"He's observing Slim at the corral. That's code for making him take a break. That boy never stops, so I have to create opportunities for him to rest. He wants to please everyone."

Trevor was right. Cole expended a lot of energy trying to please the adults in his life. He probably should see a therapist at some point. Right now, what the cowboy was offering him was even better. Consistency and friendship. She had to admit that while his approach was similar to hers, he'd had faster results. Trevor *was* good with kids.

"What's Gramps up to?" he asked.

"I convinced Gus to take a nap."

"A nap? Like he's a five-year-old?"

"Would you please lower your voice?" She grabbed a spatula and removed the cooled cookies from the sheet, placing them on a plate. "He's eighty-two years old, recovering from hip-replacement surgery. I'm a little concerned about him."

"You are?" The cowboy's face paled.

"He's a bit depressed. Not clinically depressed. More like…sad. Having to slow down has been hard on him." She lowered her voice. "I can't help but think that maybe he feels like he's let his family down."

"Whoa. Maybe you could explain that last part."

"Your grandfather carries a rather large burden. He feels the obligation to keep all the plates spinning for you and your brothers." Hope often found herself in awe of the Morgan patriarch, wondering if things would have been different if she'd had a Gus in her life.

Trevor scrubbed a hand over his face. "He told you that?"

"Not in so many words. But it's obvious your grandfather is a very social person, and he's missing his interactions on the ranch and in town. Before surgery, he was able to quietly check on all his grandsons and those he cares about. Now, he's isolated, a little lost and feeling guilty about it as well."

He stared at her, his expression soft and his eyes warm.

"What?" Hope asked.

"I'm impressed at how well you understand my grandfather."

"He's a very intuitive and kind person. You and your family are fortunate to have him in your life."

"I agree," Trevor said. "So tell me. What do you suggest?"

"He's agreed to start joining the ranch hands for lunch

like he used to, starting on Monday. I've called and re-scheduled his physical-therapy appointments. From now on, they'll be an hour earlier."

"Great. Great."

"There's a meeting of the town council next week. Gus and I will have dinner in town and stay for that. If you don't mind keeping Cole."

"No problem." He looked at her. "I sure appreciate this."

"It's my job."

Trevor eyed her. This time his gaze seemed oddly gentle. "You love your job."

"Of course, I do."

"I don't get it. People die. That has to be hard."

"Death is a part of life." She cocked her head. "It's a reality you face on the ranch every day."

"Yeah, but it's different with people." Trevor turned and looked out the window toward the pasture, his expression unreadable. "You aren't afraid of death, or the death of people you care about?"

Her heart clutched at the question, but she had to be honest. "I have comfort in knowing where I'll spend my everlasting and I try to make sure those I care about do as well."

"Good answer," he said softly. "Except I don't buy it. Everyone is afraid of death."

"I disagree. Everyone is afraid of losing the people they love. That's the scary part."

"Maybe so," he murmured. "Once you lose it all, it does make you gun-shy."

"Yes," she said with a nod. Gun-shy. That was exactly right.

He turned to face her. "I have a hard time wrapping my head around the fact that you do this job on purpose."

"I don't know what to tell you. I consider what I do to

be more than a job. It's an honor." Hope raised a shoulder and dropped it. "Maybe it's a calling. Like your calling."

"I don't have a calling," he scoffed. "I manage a ranch."

"Your grandfather thinks you do, and I agree. You have a calling to kids. Your heart feels their needs and their pain. It's your ministry. That's why you invited Cole to stay."

"I invited you as well."

"Not that you had much choice."

He smiled, and Hope lost her train of thought.

That smile.

She was right in her original assessment. It was his secret weapon.

"What's wrong?" he asked.

"Nothing. Nothing." She fiddled with the edge of the plate, avoiding his gaze as her pulse returned to normal.

Silence stretched between them for a moment. Finally, she looked up to see him watching her. "Bess calls you a bit of sunshine," he said quietly.

Her heart warmed. She enjoyed being around Bess. "You say it like it's something bad."

"No. I just don't get it. You deal with death and dying. Why are you always smiling?"

"It's a choice. I choose to be happy." She offered him the smile he'd commented on.

"How can I choose to be happy, Miss Sunshine?"

"Oh, it's as simple as that smile you brought out of hiding a few minutes ago. You could do it more often."

The cowboy opened his mouth and then closed it.

Hope nearly laughed aloud. She'd rendered the big man speechless. She picked up the plate of cookies and offered them to him. "Have a cookie."

He frowned and took several with his unbandaged

hand. "Uh, thanks." He held up his other hand. "And thanks for this."

"Anytime."

He looked at her, and once again, she had the feeling he wanted to say more but held back.

Hope's eyes followed him as he walked out of the kitchen. She didn't know how it happened, but it seemed that the gap between her and the cowboy had narrowed.

They weren't so different after all. Both had had the rug pulled out from under them, and now, in their own way, they were simply doing their best to carry on.

As soon as he finished off the last cookie, Trevor texted Jim to send Cole to the office. Delicious cookies. Nice big chunks of white chocolate. Hope knew her way around an oven. He'd give her that.

Still, he couldn't help but notice that she was the second woman of late who seemed to think he needed sweetening up. Hope had practically shoved those cookies at him.

It occurred to him that maybe, in another lifetime, he might have been interested in someone like Hope Burke. She wasn't anything like Alyssa. That was for sure. Alyssa was sweet and a bit lost in an adorable way. When he'd met her, he'd felt lost too—they'd needed each other.

Hope didn't need anything except her nephew. She was like a tree that withstood the storm. Or maybe she *was* the storm. For now, he figured he ought to maintain his guard around the ridiculously cheerful nurse. Something inside him whispered that she could be very dangerous to his well-being.

"Jim said you wanted to talk to me, Mr. Morgan?"

Cole stood in the doorway, his shirt damp with perspiration and his face streaked with dirt and sweat.

"You can call me Trevor or Mr. Trevor. Okay?"

"Yes, sir."

"That works too." Trevor waved him into the office and pulled a couple of bottles of water from the mini fridge. He put one on the desk and tossed one to Cole, who easily caught it. "Have a seat."

The boy cracked the seal on his and took a swig before he settled in the chair.

"Be sure to stay hydrated. It's hot out here. Keep your water bottle close."

"I will."

Trevor opened his desk drawer and handed Cole a phone. "This is yours. Here's the box. It has the charger cord and stuff inside."

Cole's jaw dropped. "A phone?"

"This is a business phone. Do you know what that means?"

"It's for business?"

"That's right. Only business. The phone belongs to the ranch. It's a tool for you to use to do your job here. It's not a toy. All the ranch wranglers are assigned one. You're a member of the Lazy M team, so you should bring yours to work every day, fully charged. Like your boots and your work gloves. This phone is part of the job."

Cole nodded, straightening to his full height at Trevor's words. "Yes, sir."

"I don't have to tell you that the Lazy M is a big ranch, and I have to be able to reach you. You have to be able to reach me as well. This phone is your lifeline in an emergency. I programmed important ranch numbers and the nonemergency number for the Homestead Pass Police Department. You can use it as an alarm clock as well. Come Monday, we'll be starting our day earlier to avoid the heat of the day." Trevor paused. "Any questions?"

"No, sir."

"A word of advice. Keep it in your back pocket. And always take it out when you drop your drawers."

"Yes, sir." Cole looked at the phone in his hand with a mixture of awe and delight. "Thank you, Mr. Trevor."

"You're welcome." Trevor stood. "That's it. We're all done for today. You can head on down to the main house."

"But it's only three o'clock."

"Occasionally, we get caught up around here. Not very often, so don't get used to it."

Cole offered a solemn nod and looked at Trevor. "Am I doing a good job?"

The unspoken question filled the silence. The kid was concerned he was going to be asked to leave if he wasn't up to snuff. The thought nearly broke Trevor's heart.

"You're the best wrangler trainee we've had around here in a long time."

The boy's face lit up at the words.

"By the way, I'm going to talk to Jim about obedience class."

"For me?" Cole reared back in stunned surprise.

"No." Trevor started laughing. "For that wily pup of yours. Jim will teach you how to follow up on training." He looked around. "Where is Patch, anyhow?"

"I cooled him down with the hose. He's sleeping in the shade."

"Great. Now about that obedience stuff."

"He needs it. My aunt gets pretty annoyed when he plays hide-and-seek while she's trying to leash him."

"Between you and Jim, Patch will soon be a little

gentleman. No worries." He chuckled. "Oh, and Gramps and I will pick you up tomorrow around ten a.m. to take you to town. We're heading to Ben's."

"Who's Ben?"

"Ben? Why Ben is a legend in Homestead Pass. He's the barber."

"I'm getting a haircut?" Cole pushed sweaty strands of hair away from his face. "My hair isn't long."

"It's summer in Oklahoma. Short hair keeps you cool. It's a health issue."

Cole sighed.

"It's hair, son. The thing is…it grows back." He glanced at the clock above the door. "You best get up to the house. Your aunt made cookies, and they're really good."

"Yes, sir!"

Trevor heard Patch bark and the fading voice of Cole as he raced away from the stables. Maybe he'd call it a day as well. He'd check his email and review the upcoming schedule for the holiday week first. Ten minutes later, Hope appeared in his doorway.

She was mad. Her cheeks were a fiery pink, and her bangs were askew, as though she'd hustled to get to his office. It occurred to him that she was even prettier than usual. He pushed away the thought and prepared for the storm.

Hands on hips. Uh-oh.

"Can I help you?" he asked.

"Who gave you permission to give Cole a phone?"

"It's required for the job."

"A phone? A phone is required?" She all but rolled her eyes and gestured toward a chair. "Do you mind?"

"Can't say that my minding would make any difference."

Hope dropped into the chair. "I'm going to take the

high road here and give you the benefit of the doubt. You've never had a child of your own. There are certain unspoken rules."

Trevor raised a palm. "I hate to start this discussion by contradicting you. I work with kids. I understand the rules. They don't apply here. The reality is that Cole is shadowing me on the ranch this summer. That makes him like staff, and all the staff are provided with phones. There are more hazards than you might imagine around here. He needs a way to reach out in case of an emergency."

"I assumed he'd always be where you can see him. I've entrusted my nephew to your care."

"He's not a baby, and I'm not babysitting." He sighed. "And he might be my son. Of course, I'm looking out for him. But Cole is nearly twelve. Boys are curious and they wander off. We can't cover them in Bubble Wrap. Stuff happens."

Hope leaned back in the chair and crossed her arms, her lips a thin line.

"I apologize," he said. "It was never my intent to disrespect you. As I said, all the Lazy M Ranch wranglers get a phone when they're hired on. It's a system we put in place when I took over as ranch manager."

She nodded. "I appreciate the explanation. It does make sense. However, I would like you to discuss things that involve Cole with me ahead of time."

"Yes, ma'am. I can do that."

"Thank you." She stood. "Have a good weekend."

She moved out of his office as fast as she'd entered it, nearly sideswiping Jim on her way. "Oops, sorry."

"No problem." Jim eased into the chair Hope had vacated. "I thought tornado season was over."

Trevor chuckled. "Apparently not."

"Takes quite a gal to stand up to the boss. Half the wranglers wouldn't have the guts to come in here and give you grief. The other half aren't that smart." He raised his brow. "You may have met your match."

"Were you eavesdropping?"

"God blessed me with superhuman hearing." Jim put a hand to his spectacularly large ears that stuck out from beneath his battered, straw cowboy hat. "Nothing I can do about it."

"I'd appreciate it if you'd zip your lips."

"About the phone or the part where you said Cole might be your son?"

Trevor grimaced and ran a hand over his chin. "Did anyone else hear that?"

"Only a few horses, and they're discreet."

"She thinks I'm Cole's father."

Jim clucked his tongue. "And?"

"You know that I went through a rough patch a long time ago. Turns out, there are a few empty hours I can't account for." He looked at the other cowboy. "Under the influence or not, I don't believe I'm the father. I'm ashamed to admit that I was a quiet drunk. Drank myself into oblivion all alone to escape my problems."

Warmth shone in Jim's eyes. "It was a tough time for everyone. Lots of folks were concerned about you, Trev." He paused. "But if you don't think you're the father, then why is Cole here?"

Trevor thought about the question for a moment. How could he adequately explain the connection he felt for the boy? He couldn't.

"Is that a hard question?" Jim queried.

"Yeah, maybe it is. I invited Cole to stay because he's a good kid who lost his mother recently. He never had a father and he's got nowhere else to be this summer." Trevor smiled. "Plus, he's a *Space Knights* nerd."

"Well, hey. That's all I gotta hear. Knighties, unite!"

"Thanks, Jim."

"No problem." He glanced around and then leaned closer. "Does your family know?"

"Nope. I'd like them to welcome Cole to the ranch because he's a great kid and nothing more for now."

"I guess you thought about a DNA test."

"Sure, and we'll get to that. But when it comes back negative, Hope will head back to Oklahoma City with him. I think he needs Lazy M Ranch in his life right now." He sighed. "The ranch is what saved me when I lost my folks. Hard work is a balm for the heart, and the ranch gives you a sense of purpose when life is confusing."

"I hear you," Jim said. "I'm grateful for the Lazy M, myself." He looked at Trevor, a question on his face. "And if the test is positive?"

"Then I'll gladly accept the responsibility and my family will be the first to know."

The lanky cowboy gave a slow nod, his lips pinched together in thought. "Okay, then. Mum's the word."

"Thanks. I appreciate that. Was there something you needed?" Trevor asked.

"I figured you'd be doing the schedule, and I wanted to remind you that I'll be visiting my sister and her family in Okmulgee over the Fourth of July holiday. You said I could take off next Thursday through Sunday."

"Yeah, sure. I have it down."

"When you get back, can you put Patch on your to-do list? Work with Cole and give them both some obedience training."

"You got it." Jim unfolded his frame and stood. "What are you doing for the Fourth of July?"

"Give me a break. You know that ranchers don't have holidays."

"No. *You* don't have holidays." He eyed Trevor. "Okay, after you finish chores, what are you going to do?"

"Requisite picnic at Drew's."

"Don't make it sound like the death penalty. You have a great family, and Sam married a chef. Doesn't sound like torture to me."

"Yeah, you're right." Trevor took a deep breath and released it slowly. "It just gets tedious with all that love in the air. Lucas isn't around to provide a distraction."

Jim laughed and nodded toward the door. "Your tornado friend going to the barn dance?"

"I heard Gramps mention it. But I don't know."

"Invite her yourself. That would provide plenty of distraction."

Yeah, that was an understatement. Hope, with her long straight dark hair and those bangs, always tousled, and her clear hazel eyes. A distraction, all right.

Trevor stood. "Well, would you look at the time. Sorry that you have to be going."

Once again, Jim's laughter rang out. "You can't run from life forever, my friend."

"Sure, I can. Watch me."

Chapter Six

Switzerland. Talk about eating your words. Hope pulled into a parking spot in front of the Homestead Pass Inn.

She'd lost her temper with Trevor yesterday. Not cool. Not Switzerland either. She was in the right, but she could have handled things more diplomatically.

Stepping out of the car and into the humid embrace of summer, she glanced up and down Main Street. No sign of Trevor's truck. Maybe it was around the block.

The barbershop was on the same side of the street as the inn, on Main, but at the other end of the block, next to a law office. All she had to do was casually make her way down the street, window-shopping. Yes, that was what she was doing. Window-shopping her way toward the barbershop because she couldn't resist a peek at Cole on male-bonding day.

As she started up the street, Hope heard her name called and turned around. Sadie and Liv Morgan were walking toward her with smiles on their faces. She'd gotten to know the two Morgan wives from when they'd show up at the house to visit Gus. Both were gracious and welcoming.

"Hi," Liv called as she approached. In jeans and a

T-shirt, her red cowboy boots clicked on the sidewalk. The vivacious brunette offered a smile.

"What are you up to today?" Sadie asked. Drew's wife seemed the more subdued of the duo.

"I'm running a few errands." *Not untrue.* "I see you're having a mom's day out," Hope said to Sadie.

"Yes. Drew has the kids, and I'm catching up on my life. Liv and I have hair appointments at the salon in a few minutes."

"I wasn't aware of a salon in town."

"Oh yes. Turn right at the corner of Main and Edison," Liv said. "It's next to the Hitching Post. The Rancher's Wife Salon. Wonderful place. They have cucumber water on tap and the best fashion magazines. Just like the city."

As they stood on the sidewalk, Eleanor from the bookstore hurried toward them, clipboard in hand. "Yoo-hoo! Hello to my favorite girls." She gave Liv, her stepdaughter, a kiss and hugged Sadie. "Miss Hope, how are you?"

Liv looked at Hope. "You two have met?"

"Yes. We met in the bookstore."

"Fundraising barn dance is two weeks away." Eleanor flipped through the papers on her clipboard. She arched an eyebrow. "Hmm. I don't see that any of you have bought tickets."

"You're right," Sadie said. "And it's for such a good cause." She pulled a few bills from her purse and handed them to Eleanor.

"Olivia?" Eleanor tapped her clipboard.

"I wouldn't miss it. My aunt is catering. Two tickets and hit my husband up for the bill."

"And you, Ms. Hope?" Eleanor shot her an expectant look.

"I don't think so. I don't even know anyone in town."

Liv put her arm through Hope's. "That's why you should attend. Besides, Colin Reilly doesn't open his ranch to the public often. The event will be outside, but you can be sure it will be fabulous."

"Colin Reilly?"

"Reilly pecan empire," Liv said.

"Doesn't ring a bell."

"His daughter, Harper, is best buds with Lucas Morgan," Liv said. She patted Hope's arm. "It will all make sense once you meet everyone. Another reason to attend."

Hope considered mentioning that she was only here for the summer. If that. But resistance seemed pointless.

"Okay. Sure." She reached for her wallet.

"No. No. My treat," Liv said. "Eleanor, we'll take two more tickets. You can charge my husband for those as well."

"That's what I like to hear." Eleanor laughed as she handed out the tickets. Then she looked across the street, where two women stood looking into the Glitz and Glam boutique window. "I see customers. Toodle-loo, my dears. Must sell more tickets."

Hope stared at the bright pink tickets in her hand. "Why two?"

"One is for your date, silly," Liv said with a smile. "We can discuss it at the Morgan Fourth of July family picnic. Drew and Sadie are hosting this year." She paused. "Gus invited you to the picnic, right?"

"Yes, but I don't want to intrude on a family event." Though she'd been touched by the older man's invitation, Hope still wasn't certain about attending.

"You're family for the summer," Liv said. "Besides, the men who work on the Lazy M adore Cole. All I hear from Sam is 'Cole this' and 'Cole that.' You have to bring him."

"I didn't realize your husband works on the ranch as well," Hope returned. "I haven't seen him."

"Ranch accountant. He mostly hides in his office and comes out for events that require all hands on deck. Actually, all the Morgan men have their fingers in the ranch activities somehow," Liv said.

Sadie put a hand on Hope's arm. "Listen, I was new to town myself two years ago. The Morgans are the-more-the-merrier type, and they mean it. Besides, it's at my house, making me the boss."

"It's a ton of fun," Liv said. "We bring out the horseshoes, and my father sets up the bocce balls. My family is coming, including my aunt Loretta. They're Morettis not Morgans." She chuckled. "The more-the-merrier theme continues."

"All right. We'll be there. Thank you so much." A warmth settled in her chest at the kindness.

"Oh, and it's a potluck," Liv said. "Bring your favorite side dish."

"I make a yummy spinach salad. Would that be appropriate?"

"Nutritious food. What a novelty. Yes, please." Liv patted her abdomen. "Our little baby Morgans would like that."

Sadie checked her watch, and her eyes rounded. "We better hustle, Liv." She smiled at Hope. "See you for the Fourth, if not sooner."

"Yes," Hope returned. "And thank you."

"Nice to see you again," Liv echoed as they headed in the other direction.

"You too."

Hope continued down the street buoyed by the conversation with Liv and Sadie. What would it be like to be part of a large loving family like the Morgans? She couldn't even imagine, but for now, she'd enjoy the hospitality and do her very best to avoid any further discussion of dates.

She stopped just before the barbershop and planned her casual stroll past. When the glass storefront came into view, she took a quick side-eyed glance inside. Her heart melted at the sight of Cole sitting in the barber's chair next to Gus. Both males had black capes around their necks as barbers attended to their hair.

Anna's boy was growing up. The moment was bittersweet.

"Hope!" Trevor's voice rang out.

Busted.

She turned. "Oh, Trevor. Hi there. I was just…"

"Helicoptering?" His lips twitched in that annoying know-it-all way.

"As a matter of fact, I'm on my way to the coffee shop."

He pointed a thumb behind them. "It's the other direction. Take a left on Edison."

"I've been there before, thank you. Getting my steps in by going around the block."

"Right." The single word conveyed his skepticism.

"Where's your truck?" she asked.

"I borrowed Drew's sedan. Easier for Gramps to get in and out of than my dually."

"Of course. I should have suggested that." Hope cleared her throat and absently removed a white piece of dog hair from her T-shirt. Courtesy of Patch.

"About… About yesterday," Hope began.

"Yesterday?" He shook his head as if confused.

"The phone thing." *Could this get any more awkward?*

"Have you changed your mind? Do you want me to get the phone from Cole?"

"No. I'm trying to apologize for overreacting before I heard your side of the story."

"Not a big deal."

"It is to me. You've been nothing but generous with your time and expertise and, well, the whole house thing." Now she was babbling.

As they stood there, a breeze moved past, bringing a fresh, clean, powdery aroma from the cowboy. His thick caramel hair ruffled, calling her attention to his head.

"Nice haircut," Hope said. Trimmed neat and short, the curls on his neck were gone, which was too bad. He'd gotten a shave too. The effect emphasized the angles of his face, though truthfully, she was partial to the stubble.

"You don't think it's too short?" He ran a hand through his hair.

"It's hair. It will grow back. I think it looks great." Hope glanced away, adjusting her purse on her shoulder.

Trevor laughed, and she looked up. "What's so funny?" she asked.

"I told Cole the same thing about hair growing back. I guess we're on the same wavelength."

That, she doubted.

"Did you see Cole?" he asked.

"Yes. I've never seen him happier. He looked like he was having a great time. Thank you."

"Nothing I'm doing. Just let him be a kid."

"It's not just that. You're not treating him like a kid. You treat him with respect, and you listen to him. You have expectations, and you're confident he won't disappoint you. He senses that."

Trevor's blue eyes flashed with surprise. "I think that's the nicest thing you've ever said to me."

"Don't let it go to your head."

"I just might." He offered a small smile.

"What kind of haircut for Cole?" she asked. "I mean, how short? One or two inches." Hope nodded, waiting for his agreement.

"Oh, he's getting the summer special."

Hope looked at him. "Summer special?"

"Buzz cut."

"A buzz cut?" She was more than a little surprised. Cole liked to hide behind his hair. "He's okay with a buzz cut?"

"Sure. It'll keep him cool."

"He agreed to a buzz cut?" That didn't sound like Cole at all.

"We discussed the pros and cons, and he made his own decision." Trevor shrugged. "I might have sweetened the deal with the promise of a straw hat like mine after the haircut."

Her jaw sagged. "You bribed him?"

"Not at all. Cole needs a hat regardless." He shrugged once again. "I like to think of it as synchronicity."

Synchronicity. That was a stretch. "I could have gotten a hat for Cole," she said.

Trevor narrowed his gaze. "Have you ever shopped for a cowboy hat before?"

"No."

"Then why not leave it to the experts? Besides, Gramps is looking forward to giving his opinion. He's also looking forward to restocking his horehound candy supply while we're there. You don't want to disappoint my grandfather, do you?"

"No." Hope paused. "Thank you," she said softly.

"My pleasure. We plan to stop at that new burger place outside town for lunch. Care to join us?"

"Oh, no." She raised a hand. "I don't want to intrude. Enjoy your day."

Trevor raised a brow. "You enjoy your walk."

Her walk. It was a long one. Around the block and up Parker Road, before turning left on Edison.

As she was about to walk into the coffee shop, Pastor McGuinness walked out. The tall, gray-haired pastor offered a bright smile.

"Ms. Burke," he exclaimed. "Good to see you. I tried to catch you on Sunday, but you walk much faster than I do."

She stepped aside to let customers enter the coffee shop. "I'm sorry, Pastor. What can I do for you?"

"The church is looking for a few youth volunteers to help with vacation Bible school next week. It's only a few hours each morning. Do you think Cole might be able to help us out?"

"Sounds like a nice change of pace from the ranch. I'll ask him and give you a call."

"Thank you so much, my dear." He turned to the door. "Let me get that for you."

A welcome blast of cool air greeted Hope as she entered the shop. She stepped up to the counter, and the same young barista as her last visit greeted her with a smile.

"Vanilla latte, right?"

Hope blinked at the woman. "You remembered."

"I did." She laughed.

"May I have it iced today?"

"Absolutely."

Hope carried her order to the same booth as last time and settled close to the window, where she could people-watch. Across the street, several women she'd met at church entered the library with their children. She found herself pleasantly surprised at how many of the folks strolling up and down the street she recognized.

Homestead Pass was a lovely town. It was a town to settle down in and raise a family, like the Morgans had. She often wondered how different her life might be if her mother hadn't died. All the rituals of everyday family life disappeared when her mom passed. Holidays were just another day. And if she didn't remind her father, he'd forget her birthday as well. When he remarried, holidays resumed, except now she was the odd person out, on the outside looking in. Once her father officially adopted Anna, it was as though Hope didn't exist.

It was fine. All good. She'd gotten by and had a satisfying life now. Her job blessed her beyond measure. She had a nice little apartment and friends from work. The home health company and her patients were her family.

Still, deep inside she was only too aware that it wasn't the same as real family.

Hope wanted so much more for Cole. The Morgans offered him more. Trevor was a good man, despite his gruff exterior. A good man who had already lost so much.

Her opportunity for a happy childhood disappeared once her mother died. Was she foolish to hope for a happy ending for her nephew? An ending she'd never had?

She'd gotten to know Trevor well enough to realize that she'd be okay with Cole living permanently with the cowboy. She could visit regularly, which would be more than she had when Anna was alive.

But what would happen if the testing was negative? Now that Cole knew why she was in Homestead Pass, how would she explain things if she didn't find his father? The conversation about finding his father had been difficult. Explaining that she'd failed would be even harder.

Hope rubbed her temple. One step at a time, she reminded herself. That's what Trevor said. She wasn't on this journey alone. The Lord had her back.

"Need any help?" Trevor called to Drew.

"Naw, I've got it." Drew dumped a bag of charcoal into the grill and stepped back from the flying cinders. He dusted off his hands and turned to Trevor. "I won't start cooking until Gramps declares himself the horseshoe champ."

Trevor couldn't hold back a laugh. Gramps held strong opinions regarding horseshoes. A glance overhead confirmed a brilliant blue sky with fluffy cumulus clouds. Perfect weather for the Fourth of July.

He grabbed a can of soda from a big tub stocked with ice and beverages, then pulled the tab. As he downed a swig of the cool liquid, snatches of conversation drifted to him, and his ears perked.

"Find you a date…" That came from Liv.

A date? Who was she talking to? A niggle of concern had him walking closer to the house where Liv, Sadie and Hope were seated on Drew's deck beneath large, colorful, sun-blocking umbrellas. Even little Mae sat in a miniature lawn chair with the ladies.

"It's going to be a wonderful event. I'm so glad…" That was Sadie chiming in. Except he couldn't hear all her words.

The clang of metal rang out, and Trevor turned. Across the yard, Gus offered Cole instructions on how to toss horseshoes as they warmed up for the annual family competition.

"The secret is in the wrist," Gramps said, holding a horseshoe. He stretched out his arm and narrowed his gaze, preparing to pitch as he focused on the stake in the pit. "You want to hit that stake. It's great to get a ringer. Three points. But touching the stake is good too. That's one point."

"How many times do we do this?" Cole asked.

"Twenty-five innings in a game."

Cole jerked back. "That's a long time, Mr. Gus."

Gramps put a hand on Cole's shoulder. "Nah. Time flies when you're winning. You'll see."

Trevor chuckled. The real secret was keeping an eye on his grandfather's foot action. Gramps had some stealth moves involving the foul line that might not exactly be legit. They'd spent many a fine afternoon loudly discussing dead ringers. But he'd let Cole figure that one out himself.

"How's it going, Trev?"

He did an about-face and found Sam approaching with a mischievous look on his face. "What do you mean?" Trevor asked.

Had Hope mentioned the paternity thing? Surely not. She was the one who had insisted on keeping things quiet. Maybe Jim had leaked the information. He sure hoped not, as it wouldn't help his overtures to become friends with Cole's aunt.

"Ease up there, buddy." Sam grinned. "That was a friendly conversation starter. No pressure."

"In that case, it's going fine." He looked at Sam. Really looked at him. His brother was always smiling these days. The crinkle lines at the corners of his eyes were permanent fixtures.

"What?" Sam raised his hands in question.

"Can't help but notice how happy you are."

"Oh yeah. Got me there. True love." Sam paused, his face stricken. "I didn't mean… Aw, Trev, that was inconsiderate of me."

"Cut it out. You can't go around walking on broken glass with me. I'm happy for you. You deserve this."

Sam's eyes softened. "Thanks."

"Excited about becoming a father?"

"Terrified. My heart starts thumping a mile a minute when I think about bringing a child into the world. At the same time, I thank God every single day for this blessing."

"How come you're terrified?"

"Aw, come on. Drew herded you and Lucas when we were growing up. I wasn't much help. What do I know about parenting?"

"It's all common sense."

Sam chuckled. "According to Gramps, common sense isn't all that common these days."

"True. However, you are aware that Sadie has an entire library of baby books, right? Borrow a few."

"Are you kidding? I already have." Sam cocked his head. "I don't know how you find it so easy working with kids."

"Maybe because I'm a big kid."

"Nah, that's not true. You've been an adult all your life. Independent and bossy. Gramps told me you walked to the nursery from the delivery room."

"Gramps may be exaggerating," Trevor said.

"I don't think so. I can't remember a time you weren't responsible."

Trevor could. He remembered a time, and it still haunted him. He cleared his throat. "Look, the truth is I was plenty nervous last year when the school bus showed up for the first Kids Day event. Then I remembered two things. I've worked with kids before. At church. We all have. The most important thing is that I'm doing what the Lord put in my heart." Trevor gave Sam a soft shoulder punch. "Same is true for you. You and Olivia are right where the good Lord wants you to be. All you have to do is trust that He will equip you for the job He called you to do."

"I'll try to remember that," Sam murmured.

Women's laughter rang out, and both men glanced over at the deck area. "Hope has sure stepped up to help in Bess's absence," Sam observed. "Hiring her full-time was a smart move, Trev." That mischievous look he'd come over with was back.

"Thanks." He'd had the same thoughts of late.

"I like Cole too. Good kid."

"Sam, we're starting," Eleanor called from behind them.

"Want to join us for bocce?"

Trevor counted heads. Eleanor. Olivia's father and her aunt, Loretta. "Nah, you've got your teams."

"You could take my place." Sam raised his brow. "I'd do that for you."

"No way. Those Morettis take their bocce way too seriously. Last time I played, your wife's daddy made me glad looks couldn't actually kill."

Sam laughed. "Anthony is all bark."

"So you say."

"Trevor," Olivia called. "Could you come here?"

"What do you know?" Trevor grinned. "I'm being summoned."

"Once again, your timing is excellent, little brother."

"It's a gift."

"Trevor?" Sam's wife called again.

He headed toward the deck and saw panic on Hope's

face. *Uh-oh. Better come to her rescue.* Though he wasn't anybody's knight, it was his duty to step in as she was new to Morgan-family dynamics.

"Coming." He hurried toward the women and climbed the steps to the deck.

"We need to find Hope a date for the barn dance," Olivia announced.

We? He rubbed a hand over his chin. "Is that right?"

"Yes. You're a guy. You know guys," she continued. "Who's a good candidate?"

There wasn't anyone in Homestead Pass equal to the task. Though it wouldn't be wise to say that aloud.

Trevor snuck a peek at Hope, whose worried gaze moved between the Sadie and Oliva. Yeah, he'd be worried too, if his fate was in the hands of his brothers' wives.

"What about Jim?" Sadie asked. "He's such a gentleman. And look how good he is with animals."

A horrified expression crossed Olivia's face. "Jim lives with his mother."

"To be fair, his mother lives with him," Trevor said. "He bought that house and has already paid it off." Trevor felt obligated to defend his buddy, though there wasn't a chance he'd let Jim date Hope.

"Trev's right." Drew had joined them on the deck. He leaned against the rail and nodded. "You can't discount a man who owns real estate."

"I agree," Sadie chimed in. "In this economy, living with your mom is not a reason to cross him off the list. Besides, Trevor lives with his grandfather. Same thing."

Whoa! Not the same thing. Trevor opened his mouth to defend himself and thought better of the idea. Best for him to stay on the sidelines of this conversation. He didn't want anything to do with setting up Hope with one of his buddies. For some reason, the thought only irritated him.

"Steve Keller is single," Sadie said. "A man in uniform has universal appeal."

"The police chief?" Drew shook his head. "No, he's hung up on Melissa from the post office."

Sadie looked at her husband. "Oh? Surely we can help the situation along."

Drew cringed. "Maybe we can talk about it later."

"What about Hank Garrett?" Olivia gave a dramatic sigh. "He's awfully cute."

Handsome Hank. Trevor barely resisted rolling his eyes, and Drew offered a snort of disgust.

"I don't think Hank is in town anymore," Trevor said. "He got a position in Arkansas at a bird sanctuary."

"Really? Okay. No Hank..." Olivia pursed her lips in thought. "What about Lucas?"

"Luc won't be home until August," Drew said.

Lucas. Not a good idea. Sure, his twin would have taken Hope to the barn dance in a heartbeat. His brother was a charmer. Women swooned in his presence, and he enjoyed his title as one of the most eligible bachelors in Homestead Pass. Oh yeah, Luc would gallantly offer to take the prettiest single woman in town to the dance. Trevor tensed at the thought as he glanced at Hope.

Her silky straight hair touched her shoulders, and the red, white and blue sleeveless blouse she was wearing with navy shorts showed off golden skin, tanned from outdoor excursions with Gramps. A smile touched her lips as her gaze moved between Sadie and Olivia. And though she appeared calm, he recognized the little wrinkle between her eyes that signaled anxiety.

He didn't blame her. His brothers' wives were playing roulette with her life.

"Trevor, did you hear me?" Olivia asked.

"Ah, sorry. I was thinking."

"Why don't you accompany Hope?" She smiled sweetly, pleased with herself. "You know. As friends. It's the perfect solution."

Fear shot through Trevor. He tugged on the neck of his T-shirt, then took a long swig of soda. Hope sat very still, her fingers tracing the webbing on the arms of the aluminum beach chair. Any answer except "yes" would humiliate her.

Head down, Trevor studied the ingredients on his pop can. "Uh, yeah. Sure." He raised his head in time to see the nonverbal exchange between his sisters-in-law. For a moment, everything froze, and then he put the pieces of the puzzle together.

I've been set up.

Set up by his brothers' wives, and he'd fallen for it like a rookie.

"You don't have to escort me," Hope said quietly.

Trevor raised a shoulder, as nonchalant as can be. "Happy to do my part for charity."

Olivia gasped, while Hope's hazel eyes flashed with surprise.

"The barn dance." Trevor's tongue tangled as he worked to get the words out. "It's a fundraiser for charity. I'm happy to do my part for the clinic."

Hope stood, her face pink. "I think I'll check on Cole." She moved right around him, down the deck steps and across the yard, her back straight.

"Way to step in it," Drew murmured.

All Trevor could do was groan. This. This was yet another reason he preferred to sit out social gatherings. His boots always jumped into his mouth.

Now he had become the bad guy. Trevor raced to catch up with Hope. "Hey, you okay with this?"

"Oh, sure. I haven't had a pity date in a long time." She didn't break her stride.

"No. No. It's not a pity date. We're both going, and I think we're friends, right?"

She kept her eyes ahead. "Technically, you're my boss."

"Nope. Not your boss. Your checks come from the Lazy M Ranch corporation."

Hope jerked to a stop and looked at him. A grimace touched her mouth before she glanced at the deck, where the Morgan family worked to pretend they weren't watching. "That is not what you said."

When she didn't respond, he released a breath of frustration. "Look, this caught me off guard. I haven't even thought about the word *date* in a very long time. I'm talking years."

Her eyes softened as though she understood. Did she? Had Gramps talked to her about his past? Suddenly it occurred to him that maybe he was the one who'd be the pity portion of any date with Hope.

"What are your thoughts on going as friends?" Hope asked.

His gaze skimmed her heart-shaped face, the tiny overbite and her full lips, and he felt the pull of attraction. And why not? Hope was lovely and nice. He'd noticed that, of late, he'd even begun to let down his guard around her.

It was as though he was waking up after a long slumber.

"Friends," he finally said with a slow nod. "I would like to go to the barn dance with you as friends, Hope."

"Okay. I accept."

She'd said yes, which meant that he now had his first date in over seven years, with a beautiful woman, to a dance that he'd insisted he wasn't going to attend.

Who'd have thought?

He could only pray that Jim didn't find out, or he'd find himself the punchline of his friend's jokes for weeks to come.

Hope looked around the kitchen, satisfied that everything was in order. With Gus gone for the morning, she'd had time on her hands. Plump oatmeal-and-raisin cookies were piled on a plate, covered with foil. She'd baked a chicken-and-rice casserole and tucked it in the refrigerator for Trevor and Gus's dinner.

The kitchen was spotless, and she'd even washed and dried a load of towels. It was noon, and there wasn't anything else to do except let Trevor know she was leaving.

Heading down the hall, she stood outside his office, hesitant to knock. He'd been unusually quiet since the Fourth of July picnic a week ago, and he'd been strong-armed into taking her out.

Pushing past her anxiety, Hope swallowed and gently rapped on the closed door.

"Come on in."

She turned the handle and peeked inside. His back was to her, his broad shoulders stretching the fabric of a navy T-shirt as he stared at a chart pinned to the wall. He turned around and flashed a quick smile. At the unexpected gesture, her heart, normally so restrained, responded with a little skip, and her breath caught in her throat.

"I'm leaving now," she blurted. "Gus is at that book-club luncheon at Jane Smith's. He made it clear I wasn't needed, and he has a ride home."

"A solo outing. So you think he's ready for that?"

"Your grandfather was quite adamant. I gave Jane my number, just in case."

Trevor nodded slowly. "Jane Smith? She used to be the librarian when I was in school." He paused. "Great to see Gramps being social, don't you think?"

"Just so you know. I think it might be a little more than being social."

"Really?" His brows shot up with surprise. "Gramps?"

"Yes." She smiled, amused at the expression on Trevor's face. The man clearly hadn't considered the possibility that his grandfather had a personal life.

"Okay, my grandfather is dating. This is good. I think." He stood and added a sticky note to the chart. "Where did you say Cole is?"

"Vacation Bible school at the church. He's a teacher's aide. I'll pick him up soon."

"Yeah. Yeah. That's right. Good for him. He's paying it forward."

She glanced at the chart. A closer look showed it to be a colorful map of the ranch. "What are you working on?"

"It's a topographic map of the layout for Kids Day."

"Oh yes. I noticed signs in church on Sunday. Coming up, isn't it?"

"Coming up way too fast. It's in August. This is the second year, so hopefully, all the glitches are behind us. Volunteers from the church signed up long ago. Olivia's restaurant donates box lunches. I have wranglers signed up for different ranch events with the kids. Sam and Drew are my ground team, handling generators, portable restrooms and such. Sadie is the point of contact for the few vendors we have. And the church staff is taking care of the crafts tent."

"Vendors?"

"The kids get tokens when they arrive, and they can earn them at each event. The tokens can be turned in at a vendor booth for prizes like books, games, treats."

"What a fantastic idea."

"Yeah. I can't take credit for that. It was Lucas's idea. This is the first year to implement that system."

"I think it's genius."

"Luc saw something similar at a kids' rodeo up in Montana."

Hope nodded and pointed to the wall. "What are all those colorful squares?"

He glanced between her and the map. "Each of these squares represents an event. This red cross is the medical tent. I have a nurse from Homestead Pass Elementary School coming and the local ambulance service is on standby."

"Having a medical tent is very wise." She nodded with approval. "Tell me more about the events."

"A couple down the road will bring miniature horses for rides, and I'm working on a petting zoo." Trevor pointed to different squares. "There's fishing in a barrel. Rubber-dart archery. We even have a hay maze race." He grinned, obviously excited to share the details. "Oh, and Jim teaches roping using a dummy steer. We even have a class on how to feed chickens and collect eggs. They love that."

"That sounds like fun...and a lot of work."

"Yeah. I'm spending a significant time in prayer because the reputations of the event, the ranch and even Pastor McGuinness are on the line. I can't let anyone down. Especially the kids."

Her heart warmed at his determination. The man really cared. "That's a lot of pressure."

"Tell me about it. Turns out I can't rest on the success

of last year. So, yeah. I'm more than a little nervous, which is why this year's prep work started months ago."

"I'm sure it will be wonderful." If there was one thing she'd learned about Trevor, it was that he was organized. "How did all this come to be, anyhow?" she asked.

"A few years ago, we had a pulpit guest from a church in Elk City. They had an event like this." Trevor eased onto the corner of his desk as he spoke. "Pastor and I got to talking, and he took it to the church board for financial approval, and we launched last year."

"How do you decide which kids to invite?"

"That, I leave to the good pastor."

"Any child would be thrilled to be part of this. It's an amazing outreach, Trevor. I know that I could have used something like this after my mother died. An opportunity to simply be a kid for the day."

A crease appeared between his eyebrows. "I didn't realize your mama passed. I'm sorry for your loss. I take it you were pretty young?"

"Yes. I was ten, and my father remarried an unpleasant woman. Anna's mother became my stepmother." She laughed at herself. "I sound like I'm poor little Cinderella."

"Not at all," he said slowly. "It sounds like this is why you empathize so much with Cole. You've literally been there."

"And so have you," she said softly.

He nodded, his gaze on the chart.

Silence stretched between them, the only sound the soft buzz from the air-conditioning vents.

Trevor's phone pinged, breaking the silence, and he looked down.

Hope gestured toward the door. "I should go."

"Sure." He raised his phone. "Confirmation for the lab appointment. Did you get yours?"

"Earlier today. Elk City."

"Mine is in OKC." He frowned. "Different locations?"

"Yes. I was told that's the protocol. You're voluntarily doing this, but many situations are contentious, so assigning different locations is appropriate."

He nodded and cleared his throat. "Are we still on for tomorrow night?"

"Yes. Of course. I hadn't planned to stand you up." She paused. "But if you need to cancel, I understand."

"Cancel? No. I wouldn't do that to you."

She nodded, searching for something to say. "There are cookies on the counter and a casserole in the fridge."

"Aw, you didn't have to do that. You're supposed to be a nurse, not a housekeeper. I mean, not that we don't appreciate it. We do. I'm getting mighty tired of my own cooking."

"You realize my nursing services may not be needed much longer, right? Your grandfather is progressing nicely," she said.

Trevor glanced at the wall calendar. "It's just over two weeks until his follow-up appointment."

"Yes, and I'm committed until then."

"Great, because it's been a huge peace of mind knowing you're at the house during the day." Trevor tilted his head and looked at her. "So if you have to bake more cookies because he's doing well, then so be it."

Hope laughed as she reached for the doorknob. She headed back down the hall, her steps light. Once she was outside on the porch, she stopped and glanced around at the bustle of ranch activities. The air smelled of the musky scents of animals, dirt and the Oklahoma sun.

In a heartbeat, she realized how much she enjoyed

the Lazy M. Yes, living here was something she could get used to.

And that concerned her because this was only a temporary stop on the road. She needed to remember that.

Chapter Seven

It had been more than a week since the picnic, and Trevor had spent every day since dreading tonight. Tonight was the charity barn dance at the Reilly Ranch.

He scowled as he looked at himself in the mirror.

Blue oxford shirt. Check.

New Wranglers. Check.

San Antonio trophy buckle. Check.

Lousy attitude. Check.

What am I doing? He glanced at the picture of himself and Alyssa on his dresser. Was he moving on? Was that what this was?

Emotion clogged his throat, and he swallowed hard. Would Alyssa understand?

Hope was a friend. This really wasn't a date. Yet, it seemed a monumental turning point.

And he was scared.

He picked up his wallet, and it slipped from his fingers. For a moment, he simply stood and stared at his shaking hands. Then he took a deep breath and retrieved the leather.

"Trevor, you're gonna be late, son." Gramps's voice echoed from the bottom of the stairs.

"On my way." He strode toward the door, flipped off the light switch and double-timed his way down the steps and into the kitchen.

Trevor's heart warmed at the sight of Cole and Gramps eating cookies and drinking milk at the table. A half-eaten package of chocolate-sandwich cookies sat smack in the middle of the table.

"You have to open the cookie and eat the cream first," Cole said. "That's the best part."

"Naw," Gramps protested. "That's for amateurs. The proper method is dunking the cookie in the milk, and then you're supposed to put the entire cookie in your mouth."

Gramps demonstrated, and Cole started laughing, slapping a hand on his leg. He was still wearing his straw cowboy hat, now perched on the back of his head. Hope said he only took it off when absolutely necessary.

"So, Cole, what are you and Gus going to do to-night?" Trevor asked.

Cole shoved another cookie in his mouth and chewed thoughtfully before answering. "He said to call him Gramps from now on."

"Okay, what are you and Gramps going to do?"

"Gramps is going to teach me to play chess."

"Wow, that's impressive."

"Quit stalling and get going." Gramps eyed Trevor and nodded toward the door. "You got this."

In response, Trevor leveled a gaze at his grandfather. "It's been more than seven years. Maybe I forgot how." Or maybe he didn't want to remember. Life was a lot safer if he didn't take risks.

"You never forget how to live life. Go get yourself back in the game," Gramps said.

"What are you talking about?" Cole looked between the two men.

"Nothing important," Trevor said. "I better go. Don't let Gramps get into the Dr Pepper while I'm gone."

Cole wiped his mouth with the hem of his white T-shirt and looked at him. "Why not?"

"Because he won't be able to sleep if he drinks too much caffeine. And if Gramps doesn't sleep, nobody sleeps."

"Aw, go on," Gramps muttered. "You're a party pooper."

Trevor chuckled as he left the duo and headed to his truck.

The setting sun cast a lavender-and-orange glow upon the horizon as he pulled up to Hope's house. Trevor paused. Hope's house? How had that happened? But it was more her house than it had been anyone else's. She'd put her mark on the place.

The woman loved pink. Pink flowers hung from baskets on the little front porch. She'd found two wicker chairs at a yard sale and painted them white and put pink flowered cushions on them. The place was welcoming now.

Trevor jumped out of his truck and took the steps two at a time to the porch.

"I was beginning to think you changed your mind," Hope said from the other side of the screen. The woman was clearly annoyed.

"Lost track of time. Sorry." He glanced at his watch. "Good not to be the first to arrive."

"I guess." Hope opened the screen and stepped outside, turning suddenly and nearly running into him. "Sorry," she murmured.

"Now we're both sorry," Trevor said.

She looked up at him and chuckled. "I'm cranky *and* sorry."

That got him laughing. "Nice to meet you."

Trevor noted her white peasant blouse, denim skirt

and boots with appreciation. What was the protocol here? Should he tell her that she looked nice, or would that cross the friends boundary line? As tempting as crossing that line seemed, it meant letting his guard down and sharing the secrets of his past. He wasn't certain he was ready for that. He stepped back and gestured for her to lead the way to the truck. When she did, her scent wafted past. "You smell like vanilla." The words slipped from his mouth without asking permission.

"It's my shampoo, I imagine. I don't wear perfume. Too many patients with allergies or sensitivities to scents."

"I never thought of that."

A thump sounded, and he looked down at Hope's purse on the ground. They both reached for it, his head inches from hers.

"I've got it," Trevor said. He scooped up the bag and handed it over.

"I might be nervous," she murmured. "And a little grouchy because I agreed to this. Nothing personal, but social events aren't really my thing."

"I understand." He opened the door and offered Hope his hand to step up into the truck.

"Thank you."

It was impossible to ignore how her hand, soft and warm, fit nicely into his. He hadn't held a woman's hand in a very long time.

"You're nervous too?" Hope asked when he climbed into the driver's seat.

"Uh-huh."

Trevor pressed the ignition button. "You and I haven't chatted about much but Cole, have we?"

She nodded. "You're right."

"Full disclosure. Small talk isn't my strength."

"Mine either." She fastened her seat belt and sat quietly as the truck's engine purred.

"You should know that this is the first time I've been on a…whatever this is since I lost my wife seven years ago. Can't say I've been very social since then." Trevor chuckled. "Not that I was social before that." He met her gaze and looked away.

"I'm sorry for your loss, Trevor." Hope cleared her throat. "Since we're being honest, Bess mentioned your, um, situation a while ago."

"And yet you still agreed to let me escort you tonight?" He gave a slow nod of respect.

"We've all got history." Hope shrugged. "It's about how that history makes us or breaks us and dictates our tomorrows."

"Well said. So how come you're nervous?" he asked.

"As I said, I'm not very social either. I'm a hot mess in situations like this."

Trevor laughed. "I get it." He fastened his seat belt. "Now that we've ascertained that we're both socially challenged, let's relax and get through the evening." He looked at her, taking in the clear hazel eyes and the hesitant smile that touched her lips. "Can't say there's anyone I'd rather be awkward with tonight besides you."

She seemed to relax at the words. "Thank you."

It felt good, to be honest. Hope was easy to talk to, and conversation flowed. He was surprised when fifteen minutes had passed, and he guided the truck through the gated drive of the Reilly home.

"Wow," Hope said. She peered out the window. "Is that valet parking in the middle of farmland?"

"Yeah. The Reillys are Homestead Pass royalty. Only the Pecan King would build a mansion here in the middle of nowhere."

"The Pecan King. Who knew?"

Before Trevor could get out of the truck, a valet opened the passenger door and offered Hope a hand to the ground.

The raw high-pitched twang of a fiddle tuning up could be heard in the distance.

Colin Reilly greeted them as they strolled up a flagstone walkway. The older man wore an impressive Stetson, and a crisply starched white Western shirt and bolo, with creased Wranglers and shiny boots. He grinned and reached for Trevor's hand.

"Trevor Morgan. I thought I was hallucinating. My wife is going to regret missing this event. Harper as well."

"Good to see you, sir." Trevor turned to Hope. "This is my friend Hope Burke."

"Pleased to meet you, ma'am. My wife was unexpectantly called out of town. Her mama isn't well."

"I'm so sorry," Hope said.

"Hope is a nurse," Trevor interjected. "She's been taking care of Gus after his surgery."

"I see. Sounds like, not only are you dating a pretty gal, but she's smart too." He grinned. "You and I should talk, Miss Hope."

"Oh?"

"Yes, ma'am. I've got some ideas you could help me with." Colin paused and shook his head. "Shame on me. My wife would be wagging her finger about now. Here I am, all ready to talk business." He gestured toward the other guests. "You two go enjoy yourselves. We'll talk another time."

"Nice to meet you, sir," Hope said.

"You as well. I'm pleased as can be that Trevor brought you."

"Sorry about that," Trevor said when they'd moved from Colin's hearing.

"What?" She looked at him.

He frowned and glanced around. "Colin assumed we're an item. Folks are going to think the same thing and I don't have the energy to explain otherwise to all of Homestead Pass. My plan is to nod and smile. That work for you?"

"Sure. We can break up tomorrow." Her lips twitched, and amusement lurked in her bright eyes.

Trevor laughed. He was beginning to suspect that Hope had a wicked sense of humor. "Yeah. Good plan."

He took her arm. "This way. Watch your step. The ground is a bit uneven out here." Glowing lights lining the pathway directed them toward the barn area, where the guests had gathered.

"Thanks," Hope said. "I'm glad I wore boots." She smiled.

"New boots?" he asked.

"Not at all. These are Ariats, and I have several others in my closet." She gave him a sidelong look. "I'm an Okie too, you know."

"I guessed you were a city girl."

"A little bit country and a little bit city. I was born in Oklahoma City, though after my mother passed, my father moved us to a dot on the map outside El Reno."

"Your father still around?"

"I'm sure he is, but he doesn't keep in touch. He took off when I was eighteen and headed back to the rodeo. He was a stock manager."

There was no emotion in her voice. No indication of how she felt about her father's defection, and Trevor couldn't help but ache for all Hope had lost. "I'm sorry," he murmured.

"There's nothing to be sorry about," she said. "That's my past. This is my present."

Somehow he doubted that was all there was to the story, but he wouldn't spoil the evening with questions. He knew what it was like to be prodded about things he'd rather keep buried. Once again he couldn't help but notice that he and Hope had a lot in common.

The sound of country music and the hum of voices got louder and broke the silence as they approached the expansive yard behind the Reilly home.

The ground lights disappeared, giving way to overhead lighting. Large globe lights strung on poles lit up more of the yard. Even more lights crisscrossed overhead to illuminate a portable dance floor that backed up to a small stage, where a country band was playing a peppy number.

An ingenious decorator had placed bales of hay covered with quilts around the perimeter of the dance floor to provide seating. To the right, a row of pecan trees wrapped with tiny white lights set a romantic scene. All around, couples stood in groups, talking and tapping their toes to the music.

"This is beautiful," Hope murmured.

"Yeah. The barn has been set up for a buffet dinner. Olivia's aunt caters events like this. I heard there's a barbecue with all the fixings."

"I'm hungry already," Hope said. "I guess you've been here for parties like this before."

"A few times. The Reillys have four daughters. Three of them are married, and their weddings were held here. Impressive events, not unlike this one."

They kept walking until the Reilly house came into view.

Hope stopped in her tracks and tipped her head to assess the classic stone colonial mansion that provided a backdrop for the evening.

"I hear it has six restrooms," Trevor said.

"Wow, that's a big house." She lowered her voice. "I like your little house better," Hope said.

"Me too," Trevor agreed, though it was nice to hear someone say it aloud.

She looked around, her eyes round as more and more people appeared. "Is the entire town here?"

"Close to it." He turned to her.

"What's that tent over there for?"

He turned toward a white tent on the other side of the barn. "Silent auction to benefit the clinic. Do you want to take a look while I find us something to drink?"

"Yes. That would be lovely. Thank you."

Hope's gaze followed Trevor. Tall and handsome, he garnered more than a few appreciative glances as he wove his way around people. She sighed, grappling with the reality that she was having more than simply friendly feelings toward the man. It wasn't all about his good looks either. Trevor was genuinely nice, with a heart as big as the corral that sat outside the stables.

All good if she was looking for a complication. Looking to need someone in her life.

She wasn't.

Hope began to turn toward the silent auction tent, then stopped when she spotted Eleanor moving quickly in her direction.

"Yoo-hoo, Hope!"

"Eleanor, how nice to see you." The older woman had on a white felt cowboy hat with a turquoise feather. Her Western outfit, complete with high-wattage bling, would get a nod of approval from Dolly Parton herself.

"I'm thrilled that you made it tonight." The older woman assessed Hope from head to toe. "That peasant blouse is adorable. Love the skirt."

"Thank you."

"Are you here alone?" She glanced around. "Or did Olivia find you a date?"

"I'm here with a friend." Hope braced herself for an interrogation.

"How nice." Eleanor smiled. Her owlish eyes lit up. "Anyone I know?"

"Trevor Morgan." She said it casually and feigned interest in the auction tent she hoped to reach soon.

"Trevor?" Eleanor released a soft gasp. "Trevor!" The older woman's face lit up with delight. "Well, isn't that something? I had no idea you two were an item."

"We're not." She offered Eleanor a bright smile and gestured around them with a hand. "Isn't it heartwarming how the entire community came out in support of the clinic?"

The diversion tactic flew straight over the woman's hat. "I'm just tickled that Trevor is finally dating again. Wait until my Bible study hears this. We've all been praying for that boy."

"No. We—"

"Eleanor, Daddy's looking for you." Liv stepped between Hope and her stepmother.

"Oh, is he? Isn't that sweet? The man can't go five minutes without me."

Liv slipped her arm through Hope's as the older woman walked away. "I hope you aren't upset that Sadie and I finagled you into attending the event with Trevor." She chuckled. "We were sort of surprised that it worked, to tell you the truth."

Hope couldn't stay annoyed with Liv. She had a heart of gold. Although two hours ago, she wasn't feeling quite so generous. "Are you and Sadie considering new career paths?" Hope asked.

"You never know." Liv leaned close. "I saw you two walk in together, and my first thought was Beauty and the Beast."

"What?" She looked at Liv. "Which of us is the beast?"

"Trevor, of course. He had quite a scowl on his face. Trust me, I've been the target of his displeasure before."

"Why?"

"Long story short, the Morgans protect their own. He thought I was going to break Sam's heart." Liv held out her hand and admired her wedding ring. "Trevor had it all wrong. I wanted Sam's whole heart forever."

"Oh, Liv. That's so romantic."

"Yes. It is." Liv smiled, her eyes warm with emotion. "What about you? What do you think of Trevor?"

"He's very nice."

"That's all?" Liv laughed. "I guess you didn't notice that Trevor, like all the Morgan men, is tall, dark and swoony."

"The Morgans employ me. I don't think it would be appropriate to notice," Hope returned.

Liar. She was only too aware that Trevor was the most handsome of the brothers.

"Just an FYI. There are at least a dozen women here who have been waiting for Trevor Morgan to return to the bachelor market again." Liv paused. "You know, if he really didn't want to bring you tonight, he wouldn't have. I have a hunch that Trevor likes you."

"We're friends."

Liv's chuckle clearly said, "Nice try."

"No. Really," Hope insisted.

"He invited you to live in his house. I think it's a little more than friends."

"Trevor likes Cole."

Liv slowly shook her head. "Oh my. You are definitely underestimating yourself, Hope."

She shrugged. "I'll be gone in a few weeks. There's no time to think about anything except my plans when summer ends."

"That's a shame. You fit in so well here. Everyone loves you, and it feels like you've been here forever."

Hope smiled at the kind words. In a short time, she'd come to care about everyone in Homestead Pass too. So much so, that she didn't want to think about goodbyes. At least not tonight.

"I think all we have to do is help Trevor to realize that you need to stay."

Hope opened her mouth to refute the statement, but Liv kept talking.

"I'll let you in on a little secret. It's been proven that the way to a Morgan man's heart is through his stomach, so don't discount the power of a great recipe. I have a few I can share."

"Liv. Where's your husband?" Trevor asked, interrupting in the nick of time. He handed a glass of iced tea to Hope.

"I should go find him. Looks like the band is about to start a new set, and I've got my dancing shoes on." She gave Hope a hug. "Remember what I said, my friend."

Trevor watched Liv walk away and turned to Hope. "That sounds important."

"She offered to share a recipe." Hope snuck a peek at Trevor. Tall, dark and swoony for sure. It had been easy to ignore how handsome he was until this evening because he was also a prickly thorn in her side.

Tonight, he'd revealed that he was vulnerable. Paired with his smile, it was a dangerous combination that left her a little weak-kneed.

Across the yard, Hope spotted a tall man waving and trying to get her attention. "Is that Jim?"

Trevor glanced over. "Uh-oh. Looks like." He nodded toward the dance floor. "Can you dance?"

"Yes," she answered, more than surprised by the question.

"Let's dance."

Trevor took her hand and swept her into the crowd. He moved them around the dance floor to a slow, sweet country song. *Swept.* That was precisely what he'd done because, as it turned out, he was a very good dancer.

"Where did you learn moves like this?" Hope asked. She cautiously raised her gaze from his clean-shaven chin to his blue eyes, heavy-lidded now, as he, in return, watched her.

It was disconcerting to realize she was close enough to smell the citrus scent of his aftershave and the mint on his breath.

"Gramps taught Lucas and me for our high-school prom. He gave Drew and Sam lessons when they were in high school too."

"Sounds like you were social once."

He shook his head. "No. I didn't attend. One of my favorite science-fiction authors was in Oklahoma City for a book signing, and I convinced Sam to drive me there."

"You were a bookworm?" She feigned shock.

"I still am, thank you very much. And proud of it. Another reason why Cole and I get along so well."

She nodded, though she knew it wasn't just books. Trevor and Cole had a connection she couldn't define.

Suddenly, Hope realized that the music had stopped. She looked around. "That was nice," she observed. Unplanned and nice.

"Very nice," Trevor said softly, his gaze intent.

"Miss Hope, you are the prettiest gal here. Though I imagine Trevor already told you that."

She spun around to see a smiling Slim Jim. "Hi there," Hope said.

The skinny cowboy glanced from her to Trevor, nodding and smiling.

Trevor frowned and offered a stiff nod of greeting. "Did you bring a date?" he asked.

"Aw, she canceled, so I brought my mom." Jim chuckled and looked at Trevor. "Guess you don't have to write that check now."

"Nope." Trevor glanced around. "Your mother is looking for you."

"Yeah. Okay. I better check on her." Jim offered Hope a short bow. "Good to see you."

Hope turned to Trevor. "Okay, what was that? I got the distinct feeling that I missed something in the subtext."

"Nothing much. Trust me." He paused. "I was remiss not to tell you how lovely you look."

"Oh, thank you," she murmured. Heat warmed her face at the words.

"You know, I just figured out something," he said.

"What's that?" Hope asked.

"When we're on the dance floor, I don't have to talk to anyone."

"Except me."

"That's right. Except you." Trevor smiled, causing a chain reaction in the vicinity of her heart.

She took the hand he offered and followed him onto the dance floor as the first notes of a slow ballad began.

Tonight wasn't turning out as she'd expected. Weeks ago, she would have never believed that she and the cranky cowboy would find middle ground on the dance floor.

Oh, that God. What a sense of humor He had.

* * *

Trevor leaned back in his chair, the sounds of the stables around him a soothing white noise. Here it was Monday, and he was still thinking about that barn dance. Thinking about Hope if he was honest.

Hope was a good listener, and they had a lot in common. He couldn't help but notice that neither of them was afraid to laugh at themselves.

And it sure didn't hurt that she was easy on the eyes.

Twice this morning he'd started on paperwork and got distracted thinking about holding her in his arms on the dance floor. Each time, he'd gotten up and started for the main house, with a paltry excuse to see what she was up to today. Then he'd lose his nerve and sit back down.

"I am so lame," he muttered. He stood again and headed out of the stables, only to run into Jim.

"Hey, boss." Jim chuckled. His friend was obviously eager and ready to razz Trevor about taking Hope to the dance.

"Don't even," Trevor said while showing him a palm. "Not one word."

Jim laughed and kept walking.

"Keep an eye on Cole," Trevor called out. "He's in the tack room, cleaning saddles."

"Yes, boss. Sure will." He chuckled again.

As Trevor strode to the house, he realized Hope's car was gone. This wasn't a physical-therapy day, so maybe she'd gone into town. Just as well. He had no clue what he was going to say to her, anyhow.

He stepped into the front entry and was enveloped by cool air and the sweet aroma of cinnamon and butter. "Gramps?"

"Nobody here but us," Sam called out.

Trevor moved down the hall to the kitchen and found Sam and Drew seated at the kitchen table with coffee and cinnamon rolls in front of them.

"Hope took Gramps to Elk City today to visit the big sports store," Drew said.

Trevor nodded absently. His attention was riveted on the pan of cinnamon rolls on the counter. "Where'd you get these?"

"Cinnamon rolls?" Sam grinned. "Pulled them out of the freezer yesterday to thaw. I figured this was the perfect time to get them in the oven."

"I didn't even realize Bess had cinnamon rolls in the freezer," Trevor said.

"Yep. If everyone knew about it, they wouldn't last long, would they?" He offered a wink.

"True." Trevor grabbed a plate and helped himself to a plump roll. Then he glanced warily at the coffee maker. "Did one of you two make the coffee?"

"Yeah," Drew said. "You're safe."

Gus Morgan's coffee was legendary, and not in a good way. Gramps claimed that his coffee put hair on your chest, while Trevor and his brothers were pretty certain it burned a hole in your gut.

Trevor slid into the chair opposite his brothers.

Sam leaned back and eyed him. "Saw you on the dance floor Friday."

"So did most of Homestead Pass," Drew added.

"Uh-huh." Trevor bit into his cinnamon roll, savoring the blend of butter, cinnamon and cream cheese. For a moment, he could forget his brothers were talking.

"You and Hope." Sam cocked his head, waiting for a response.

"We're friends."

"Trevor, we don't mean to butt into your personal

business," Drew began. "I usually leave that to Gramps, but if you're under the illusion that you and Hope are just friends, you're mistaken."

"I don't want to talk about it." Nope. He wasn't going to discuss Hope with anyone. What was there to discuss, anyhow? It was too new, and he wasn't even sure what "it" was yet.

Drew looked at Sam and nodded. Dread pushed at Trevor.

"What's the deal with Cole?" Sam asked.

Trevor jerked up in his chair, alarmed at the question. "You two have a problem with Cole?"

"No. Of course not. He's a great kid." Sam shook his head. "But something's going on and we'd like to know what it is."

"What he said," Drew chimed in.

"You two sound like Gramps."

"We already asked Gramps," Sam said. "He said he doesn't know."

Drew crossed his arms and leaned back in the chair, until it rested on two legs. "You may as well spill the beans. We're not leaving until you do. You know we don't do secrets in this family."

Trevor stared at his cinnamon roll with longing. The sooner he got this over with, the sooner he could go back to enjoying his pastry. Besides, Drew was right. They didn't do secrets. He should have never agreed to Hope's request to keep this confidential. Somehow, he'd have to make her understand.

"Well?" Sam asked.

"My name is on Cole's birth certificate."

Drew's chair fell back with a bang. *"What?"*

Sam did a double take. "Cole is our *nephew*?" He beamed.

Trevor glanced around quickly. "Could you lower your voice?"

"Could *you* answer the question?" Sam asked.

"I don't know anything until the DNA testing is complete. Until then, you two are going to have to keep your mouths shut and keep your questions in your back pocket. I'm not going to discuss it further."

He should have known his brothers would be more excited about adding Cole to the family tree than about knowing the circumstances of any indiscretion he may or may not have committed.

"Huh. How about that?" Sam mused. "I knew there was something awesome about that kid."

Trevor glared at him. "Am I going to have to duct-tape your mouth?"

"What's the big deal?" Sam shot back. "I'm excited."

"This is a delicate situation. Cole doesn't know and I've already broken my pledge to Hope. That's the deal."

Drew shook his head solemnly. "I sure hope you know what you're doing."

"Let me assure you, I do not," Trevor admitted. "Feel free to add me to your prayers."

"Yeah. For sure," his oldest brother murmured.

"All right then." Sam stood, then took his plate and mug to the sink. "Carry on in the proud tradition of Morgan men who also have no clue what they are doing."

Drew stood and released a whoosh of air. He grabbed his Stetson from the wall hook and slapped it on his head. "Good talking to you."

Trevor nodded and stared at his plate, his appetite now gone.

Minutes after Sam and Drew left, Trevor heard Gramps in the front hall. His grandfather stepped into the kitchen, with Hope behind him carrying half a dozen shopping bags.

Trevor jumped up. "Let me help you with those." He took the bags from her, his fingers tangling with hers.

"Oh, sorry," she murmured.

"Cranky and sorry?" He bit back a smile, remembering Friday. When she met his gaze, Hope smiled too.

"What is this?" Gramps stood next to the counter, his eyes fixed on the pan of cinnamon rolls. "Am I dreaming?" He closed his eyes and opened them again, then turned to Trevor.

"Found them on the counter when I got here," Trevor said. "Where do you want these bags?"

"Could you take them to my room, please?"

"Sure."

Trevor headed down the hall and neatly placed the bags on Gramps's bed. By the time he returned to the kitchen, his grandfather was in a chair with a cinnamon roll and a cup of coffee in front of him.

"They're still warm." Gramps frowned. "And they taste like Bess made 'em."

"Yep… What did you get at the store, Gramps?" Trevor asked.

Gus took a swig of coffee and grimaced. "Supplies for the fishing derby. A man wants to look nice when he's winning the top prize."

"Who's on your team this year?"

"About that. Turns out Hope's got her own pole, so I invited her. She picked up a pole for Cole today." He looked at Trevor. "We need a fourth. That's where you come in."

"Gramps, the last time I was on your team, you became unnecessarily agitated when we didn't win."

"I've matured since then. Besides, I have to be on my best behavior for Cole."

Trevor nodded. "All right. I'm in. But I'll hold you to a higher standard of sportsmanship this year."

"Whatever," Gramps murmured. "Could you go into town and pay the entry fee?"

Trevor laughed. "Is that why you invited me to join the team?"

"'Course not. You're Cole's mentor, and I thought this would be a good experience for both of you."

"Fine. I'll get our team registered." He glanced at his watch. "I better get back. Cole has a riding lesson soon."

"How's he doing?" Hope asked, her gaze curious.

"That boy is amazing. Tell you what. Why don't you and Cole join Gramps and me for dinner next Saturday after the fishing derby? Afterward, we'll head out to the stables and have a little show. I think it's time for you to see for yourself."

"That would be wonderful." She eagerly nodded. "Do you want me to bring something?"

"Nah," Gramps said. "We'll have our prize-winning fish for dinner."

Hope smiled. "I'll bring dessert."

"Fair enough," Trevor said. He turned to leave.

"I've got mail in my car," Hope said. "We stopped at the post office on the way in. Do you want me to grab yours?"

"Sure." He nodded to his grandfather. "See you for dinner, Gramps."

"Yes, you will. Though I probably won't be hungry once I finish this pan."

Trevor chuckled as he followed Hope out of the house to her car, where she opened the door, grabbed a stack of mail and handed it to him.

"This is the ranch mail."

"Thanks," he said, searching for something to say to fill the awkward moment.

"No problem." She paused. "Did I thank you for a nice evening last Friday?"

"You did. Maybe we could do it again sometime without the town watching."

"You want to go dancing?" Her eyes rounded.

"Naw, I thought maybe dinner?"

"How about if I invite you to dinner with Cole and me?" She looked at him, her expression hopeful as she played with the mail in her hands.

She's nervous. The observation surprised him. That she hadn't rejected him surprised him even more.

"Okay, that sounds great."

"Does Thursday work for you?"

"Sure." Trevor smiled, working to keep things cool and casual. Yeah, he could do this.

"About six?"

"Yes, ma'am." He tipped his hat. "See you then."

Trevor whistled as he headed back to the stables. He hadn't made a fool of himself, which was good. For a moment, he allowed himself to think about the future. About taking a chance again. Living life, as Gramps put it.

Then he reined in his thoughts.

Right now. Today. That was all he could handle. And that was okay.

Chapter Eight

Gramps turned from the sink, wiping his hands on his Wranglers. He eyed the self-adhering wrap on Trevor's arm. "Did you donate blood?"

Trevor removed the wrap and tossed it in the trash. "I forgot about that."

"Want some?" Gus asked as he poured a cup of coffee.

"Uh, no thanks."

Mug in hand, the Morgan patriarch stepped slowly across the kitchen and eased into a chair.

"Look at you, walking with that coffee in your hand," Trevor said. "Steady as can be."

"I've been practicing for two weeks. First time I didn't spill." He chuckled. "All thanks to Hope. The woman has a will of steel. She refuses to allow me to do things the easy way. Nope. Eye on the prize, she says."

Yeah, that sounded like Hope, all right. "Glad to see you recovering so well."

"Feeling great too. And my incision is a thing of beauty. Want to see?" Gramps stood and reached for his belt.

"No!" Trevor held out a hand. "I believe you. When's your doctor appointment? Coming up, right?"

"Yep. Shortly after the fishing derby. I expect to be cleared to drive then. Praise the Lord. I'm tired of being chauffeured everywhere I go."

Gramps pushed out a chair with his boot. "Sit a spell, and you can answer that question you sidestepped five minutes ago."

"I'm not sidestepping anything." Trevor sat. "I had lab work done in Oklahoma City first thing this morning."

"That right? Are you sick? You look fine." He leaned closer, peering at Trevor. "Why didn't you go to the clinic?"

"I am fine. It's all good." Trevor ran a hand over the vein where the tech had drawn blood.

"Seems to me that's not the whole story." Gramps narrowed his gaze. "Something is going on. Care to enlighten me?"

"What makes you think something is going on?" Trevor looked around the room. Everywhere but at his grandfather, as he silently prayed he wasn't going to have to have a heart-to-heart like he'd just had with his brothers on Monday.

"Because my big toe is twitching, which means either a tornado or trouble. Or, in your case, maybe both." Gramps shook his head. "Also, it's Thursday morning, and you're usually knee-deep in chores this time of day."

Any other time, Trevor would have laughed and distracted his grandfather. But after the trip to have his blood drawn for genetic testing, he was far from good-humored. Reality had sobered his thoughts on the drive to and from the lab. Negative or positive, he sensed that the results of the lab work would change his life forever.

Trevor took a deep breath. It was time. He'd kept

things from his grandfather long enough. "I had an appointment at a lab in Oklahoma City first thing this morning for genetic testing."

His grandfather jerked back at the words, his blue eyes, so like his own, wide with surprise. "Come again?"

"My name is on Cole's birth certificate."

Gus stared in shocked silence. "I've got no words. Day and time. Put it on the calendar."

"Yeah. I hear you," Trevor said.

"When did you discover this?"

"In June. Hope told me about a week after she arrived. After I sort of stumbled on the information."

Gramps seemed to mull the words. "That's why she came all the way from Oklahoma City to take a job in Homestead Pass. Why didn't you tell me?"

"You had enough going on recovering from surgery. I didn't want to bother you."

"Have you told your brothers?"

"Drew and Sam wrestled it out of me on Monday."

Gramps snorted. "Can't say I appreciate you telling them and not me."

"It wasn't planned."

His grandfather glanced at the kitchen clock. "Son, I've got a million questions, as you may have guessed, but Hope will be back from town shortly, so I'll make it quick."

"Fair enough."

"Cole's mama. What's the story?"

"I barely knew her."

"You think you might be Cole's daddy?"

"Technically, anything is possible. You know what shape I was in back then." He tapped his fingers on the table and shook his head.

Gramps nodded, a frown drawing his eyebrows together.

"We won't know for a few weeks," Trevor continued. "The thing is, test results won't change how I feel about Cole."

It was important that he say that aloud. He wasn't mentoring Cole because he had to but because he wanted to.

"I wanted Cole to have a summer without any strings attached. The boy lost his mother. He needs to grieve and be a kid for a while, regardless of what happens." Trevor's heart clenched as he said the words.

"I guess you'd be the one to understand that firsthand."

Trevor nodded as he straightened the place mat on the table. Drew was twenty-one when their parents died. Sam, seventeen. He and Lucas were thirteen. They were anchorless and grieving until Gramps moved in. Yeah, he did understand.

"I kinda got the idea you might have feelings for Hope. Am I right?"

"Maybe. I'm taking that slow."

Gramps gave a slow nod. "Have you told her about AA?"

Trevor folded his hands and studied them. He had his father's hands—wide with blunt nails. "Not in so many words," he murmured.

"Are you scared?"

His head shot up, and he looked at his grandfather. "Sure, I'm scared. I'm terrified."

"Why? Alyssa didn't have a problem with it."

"I…I didn't tell Alyssa."

Gramps's jaw fell. "She was your wife."

"Yep. You're right. But it was a whirlwind thing, and

I was scared that if I told her, she'd walk away. We got married, and six months later… She was gone."

"Aw, son. You need to tell Hope. Upfront and immediately."

He nodded, wrestling with the inevitability of what he had to do. For too long he'd hidden from the world, and from the secrets of his past and the truth of his battle with sobriety.

Gramps was right. There was no room for secrets. He'd been ashamed to tell Alyssa. His growing feelings for both Hope and Cole demanded his complete honesty. "Yes, sir. I'll tell her tonight."

"Tonight?"

"That's the reason I came in the house. I'm having dinner at Hope's this evening."

His grandfather perked at the words. "Why, that's great."

"Sam and Olivia will be by to join you for dinner. Olivia is cooking."

"Again with the babysitter." Gus grimaced. "Why is it that once you reach your glory years, everyone treats you like you're feeble?"

"They *want* to come by. For some reason, people actually like you."

"Strangest thing." Gramps eyed him over the rim of his mug. "Have I told you lately how proud I am of you?"

"I haven't done anything remarkable."

"Sure you have. Look what you've done for Cole. You've got that children's event coming up again. You're touching lives, Trev. Your mama and daddy would be proud."

Trevor swallowed hard. "Pastor McGuinness brings them in. I entertain them. Not a big deal."

"Now, there you go again, short-changing yourself and downplaying your ministry."

"It's not—" His grandfather shot him a look that stopped further protesting.

"Don't be bad-mouthing God's gift." Gramps's hands, weathered by age and arthritis, were wrapped around his mug as he leaned closer. "Let me ask you a question. What part of farming is the most important, do you suppose? Planting the seed? Watering? Sunshine? Or maybe harvesting?"

"Okay, Gramps. I get it." He'd heard this particular Gus Morgan parable before. Gramps always knew what to say to knock sense into him.

"Do you?" He shook his head. "You're a godly man, and you minister by example."

"I feel like a hypocrite."

"What part is hypocritical? The part where you were humbled and asking your Lord for forgiveness? Or the part where He forgave you?"

"Point taken, but I've got a long way to go before I can forgive myself for the past."

"You're wrong, son. Forgiveness for your sins is someone else's job."

Trevor shifted uncomfortably at the words and looked at his watch. "I've got to shove off."

"Okay, but you take my words with you."

"Yes, sir. I will."

As he strode down the porch steps, Hope's car pulled into the drive. Trevor waved, and she gave a friendly hit on the horn.

He stopped at the car and Hope rolled down her window. "Everything okay?" she asked. "You looked concerned coming out of the house."

"All good." Trevor nodded. "Had my lab work done this morning."

"Cole had his blood drawn this morning as well."

"What did you tell him?"

"I told him the truth. That we needed to have his lab results on file in case we found his father."

"What did he say?"

Hope stared straight ahead for a moment before turning back to him, lifting her chin so she could meet his gaze.

"Trevor, he said that he prayed you were his father." She blinked, her eyes becoming glassy. "I'm only sharing that because if you aren't his father, things are going to get more complicated. You should be aware of how much he looks up to you. Be very careful with his heart."

He sucked in a breath at her honest admission. Another confirmation that he had to level with her about his past tonight.

"It's a huge responsibility, being close to someone. I get that. I won't ever hurt him. Or you. You have my word."

Hope's lashes fluttered and she glanced away while offering a slow nod.

"I better get moving. Are we still on for tonight?" he asked.

"Yes. I'm looking forward to it," Hope said. Her face pinkened with the admission, a sweet vulnerability evident in the hazel eyes.

Trevor's heart tumbled at the sight. He smiled. "Me too." He set off again toward the stables, with Gramps's words echoing in his ears.

Yeah, his grandfather was right. He should have told Alyssa.

His feelings for Hope were new and a little terrifying, but he vowed not to make the same mistake twice.

* * *

"Aunt Hope, are you and Trevor boyfriend and girlfriend?" Cole asked as he opened the refrigerator and stared at its contents with great focus and then closed the door.

Hope blinked at the unexpected question. She'd intended to be circumspect around Trevor. Cole was going through a lot. There was no need to add more complications to his life. He needed to be able to trust that she'd never let him down or fail to put his best interests first.

She turned and looked at him for a moment. He was wearing his straw hat, as usual, and she noted he'd added a few healthy pounds to his slight frame. Though he wore sunscreen at her direction, his skin had tanned a light gold and his freckles had multiplied since they'd arrived at the ranch.

"Trevor and I are friends." She grabbed a potholder, lifted the slow-cooker lid and stirred the chicken and rice. The aroma of wild rice and savory chicken had her stomach grumbling.

"Then why is Trevor coming to dinner?" He closed the refrigerator and looked at her. "And why did you put on your nice clothes and lipstick and all?"

Hope stared at her nephew. He was much too observant. Yes, she was guilty of taking a shower and putting on a sundress and sandals. She'd even put on lip gloss. Of course, he noticed.

"It's not a date. It's dinner. Friends have dinner with each other. Remember how you and Gramps and Trevor went for burgers?"

"Are you sure? I saw him talking to you at the corral, and Jim said he's sweet on you. That means he likes you." Cole gave her a knowing look.

"I like him too. I like you and I like everyone here on

the ranch." It was time to change the subject. "So, Cole, tell me about your horseback-riding lessons. Trevor says I get to watch on Saturday after we have dinner with Gus."

"I ride Storm. He's a Appa—Appa…"

"Appaloosa."

"Yeah. That. Storm is dark brown and white like Patch. I groom him and everything. No one else rides Storm except Trevor and me. He's like my very own horse." He grinned. "Trevor said I can bring him an apple sometimes. Can we buy apples?"

Hope stared at him, concern nagging at her. First the dog and now a horse. This would complicate leaving. And they'd know if that was their next move very soon.

"Storm. Wow, that's great. Yes. I'll pick up a few apples."

"Thanks, Aunt Hope."

She put a hand on his shoulder. "Cole, you know we're only here until my job with Gus ends, right?"

"Can't we stay until school starts?" He frowned, his lower lip jutting. "You said you're going to find my father."

The heavy weight of Cole's words nearly crushed her. Hope prayed for guidance, knowing how important her response was. This was not the time to dismiss his concerns. She'd vowed honesty with her nephew, but hadn't expected it to hurt so much.

"I'm doing my best to find your father, but the truth is, we may never be able to locate him. Your mother didn't leave us with much information." She'd rather prepare him for a worst-case scenario than give him false hope about Trevor Morgan.

Confusion clouded his blue eyes.

"As for how long we stay, I don't have an answer to that yet. Oklahoma City is your home now. It's where you'll go to school. We can't stay in Trevor's house forever." Hope paused. "We have a few more weeks here. Plenty of time to enjoy Storm, right?"

"I guess," he mumbled.

She longed to tell him that Trevor might be his father, but if the results came back negative, Cole would be devastated.

"Did you know I used to ride when I was your age?"

Cole lifted his head at that admission. "You did? Did you groom your horse yourself?"

"Yes, but it wasn't my horse. Our neighbor let me ride his horse." Cole's eyes widened at the information.

"Did you muck stalls? Trevor says I'm the best mucker he ever had."

"I don't doubt that. You're a hard worker, Cole, and I'm proud of you."

"My mom rode horses."

"Yes. I knew that. She had her own horse."

"My mom was a champion barrel racer. Did you ever see her race?"

"I did. Your mom was very good."

He nodded, seeming pleased with Hope's answer.

"Here." She handed him plates and silverware. "Why don't you set the table."

"Okay."

"Your room is clean, right? Trevor might want to see where you do all that reading."

Cole grimaced. "It's kinda clean."

"Set the table, and then make sure your room is tidy, please."

"Yes, ma'am." He started walking toward the dining room.

"You walked and fed Patch, right?"

"Yes, ma'am. Patch pulled weeds with me today. He's sleeping in his kennel."

"Perfect. I'm proud of the way you handle your responsibilities, Cole. You've really stepped up to help me too."

"Aunt Hope?" He paused and looked up at her, the blue eyes wide and trusting. "Are you sure we have to leave?"

"Yes, Cole. Let's not give it too much thought right now."

He nodded and left the room, leaving Hope's heart aching for what she saw in those eyes. Cole longed for a forever home. Everything he wanted was on the Lazy M Ranch. However, she refused to make promises she wasn't certain she could keep. Lazy M was indeed a dream come true. That dream, however, was temporary.

Hope pulled out a big bowl from the cupboard. By the time she'd finished putting together a tossed salad, the doorbell rang.

Cole raced to the door before she could. Hope finished putting away ingredients, all the while listening to the conversation at the entrance.

"Why did you bring Aunt Hope flowers?" Cole asked.

"It's customary for the guest to bring a gift to the host," Trevor said. She could hear the amusement in his voice.

"Why?"

"As a thank-you for the hospitality."

"What does *hospitality* mean?"

Trevor chuckled. "Hospitality. Hmm. That's you inviting me to your home."

"Okay, I get it. So what did you bring me?"

"Cole!" Hope rushed to the door. "You didn't even

invite Trevor in." She opened the screen. "Come on in. I'm so sorry."

"He's right. Cole is my host tonight as well."

Trevor handed Hope a large bouquet of bright, cheerful sunflowers. "Wasn't sure what kind of flowers you like, but these reminded me of you." He winked. "A little bit of sunshine."

"Thank you," she breathed. Her heart clutched as she caught his gaze.

No one had ever given her flowers before. She'd remember this moment for a long time.

Trevor kneeled down and pulled his backpack from his shoulder. "Got something for you right here, Cole."

Cole inched closer to the bag as Trevor unzipped the outside. He brought out five hardcover books. "The rest of the series."

"I can borrow them?" The blue eyes rounded with surprise as he eyed the stack like they were piles of gold.

"They're yours. My gift to you."

"Wow. Thank you, Trevor."

"Hey, my pleasure." He grinned. "Always good to have another friend who's a *Space Knights* fan. We Knighties have to stick together if we're going to save the universe."

Cole grinned back. "I'm going to put these in my room."

"That was really sweet of you," Hope said when Cole left the room. "Maybe you shouldn't buy him gifts, though."

His brow creased. "Hope, they're books. I didn't hand him the keys to a car."

"You're right. You're right," she said, backtracking.

"This is about you worrying that he'll get too attached to me?"

She nodded, emotion tugging at her again. The conversation earlier with Cole and now this kindness from

Trevor overwhelmed her. What if the DNA test was negative? Where did that leave her nephew? Where did that leave her? Trevor had unwittingly scaled the walls of her heart without even knowing. She feared not just for Cole, but for herself.

"No matter what the future holds, Cole will always be my friend. Always. And friends stay in touch. Right?"

"Yes."

Trevor's eyes were full of emotion, which did nothing to reassure her that she wasn't heading straight for the heartache she'd so carefully avoided for so many years.

A timer interrupted the conversation.

"Biscuits are done." She worked to sound cheerful and headed to the kitchen.

Trevor followed her. "Something smells good."

"Slow cooker chicken and rice. Nothing fancy."

"I've had your chicken and rice. It's fancy enough for this cowboy," he said.

Dinner went quickly, with Cole practically shoving his food down, eager to get back to his books.

"Let me help with the dishes," Trevor said. He finished off the last biscuit. "Least I can do after such a delicious meal."

"No. I don't believe in doing the dishes when there's a guest in the house. They're soaking in the sink. I'll toss them in the dishwasher later." She stood. "Let's sit on the back porch and enjoy the evening."

"Mosquitos don't bother you?"

"They haven't been too bad this year."

He followed her outside, where she turned on the ceiling fan, creating a breeze.

"You did everything right with this house," she said. "I sit out here almost every night, thanks to that fan."

"I can see why. Look at that full moon."

Hope glanced at the sky where the glowing moon with

its hazy halo lit up a blanket of stars. She took a mental snapshot of the sight and tucked it away to remember when she was back in the city.

They each sank into cushioned rocking chairs, positioned at angles with a small table in between. For long minutes, Hope gently rocked, occasionally sneaking peeks at Trevor's profile in the semidarkness.

"I'm sorry you never got to live in the house as you intended," she finally said.

"Me too. But life doesn't turn out the way we planned for most of us." He turned his head and smiled. "Things are pretty good right now."

"Yes," she said softly. "They are."

A comfortable silence stretched between them. The only sound was the song of the katydid over and over. *Katydid. Katydidn't.*

"Time is moving quickly," Hope said. "August will be here before we know it."

Trevor nodded.

"How are things coming along with your event? Anything I can do to help?"

"Well, since you mentioned it. Maybe you can do me a favor."

"Sure. Whatever you need."

"I told you about the medical tent. The nurse from the elementary school called last night. She has to withdraw due to a family emergency."

"I've love to help you." Hope did a quick mental calculation. "Especially after all you've done for Cole and me. But your grandfather will certainly be given a medical release next week and won't need me. I'm in limbo until the DNA results come in." Hope paused. "I'd hate to commit and then find out I wasn't staying in Homestead Pass."

Trevor nodded as though he understood her quandary. "The event is the third Saturday in August," he said. "Why don't you take a staycation while you're in wait-and-see mode."

"A staycation?" Hope chuckled. "I can't remember the last time I took time off in my life." She did another quick mental assessment, this time of her finances. It was true she'd brought in more income as a private duty nurse than as a case manager, which meant her bank account had a cushion until the end of August.

"You know it would mean a lot to Cole," Trevor added.

"No need to pull out the violins," she said. "If you're willing to put up with me staying here until your event, I'm willing to volunteer."

"I really appreciate that. You won't regret it once you see how the kids enjoy the day."

Hope leaned back in the chair, surprised at herself. She couldn't believe she'd agreed to Trevor's proposal so quickly. That wasn't how she normally functioned. She usually took days to assess all sides of an issue before making a decision.

The exception had been coming to Homestead Pass. She'd arrived on a wing and a prayer, without a safety net.

Soon she'd go back to her orderly life. The thought was unsettling.

They sat silently rocking beneath a clear sky sprinkled with diamonds and lit by a full moon. "This is nice," Hope said. More than nice, her heart whispered.

"Yeah. You can see the lights of Drew's house from here, above those trees."

Hope stood. "Yes. I see them."

"What do you want out of life, Hope?"

She eased back into the rocker and looked at him. "Where did that come from?"

Trevor shrugged. "Since you came and I found out

Anna named me as Cole's father, I've been reevaluating my life."

"I see. Well, there isn't that much I want. Someday, I hope to have enough money saved up to buy a little house. I'd like my own garden."

He nodded. "What about you?" she asked.

Trevor turned his head toward her, his blue eyes intent. "I'm not as certain about things as I used to be," he said. "To tell you the truth, I hadn't expected you and Cole to have such an impact on my life." He looked at the sky and took a deep breath. "I'm feeling things for you that I never thought I'd feel again."

Hope sucked in a breath at his words, her heart stuttering. There was no denying that despite her good intentions, she was falling for the cowboy.

Trevor cleared his throat and shifted in his seat, looking almost pained. "The thing is, I haven't told you everything about my past and I realize that I ought to."

"I'm listening." She'd learned to remain calm and nonjudgmental when listening as part of her job as a caregiver. Inside, however, she was anything but calm. Her chest was tight, and her heart thudded. Hope held her hands tightly in her lap.

"Twelve years ago, my best bud, Wishard Mason, died. And it was my fault." He ran a hand over his face and took a deep breath. "Small rodeo outside Okmulgee. I was supposed to be hazing for him that day, but I was hungover, so someone else took my place. Wishard hit the ground wrong and took a horn to the ribs. Freak accident, really. But I should have been there. It was my job. I let Wish down."

Hope knew enough about rodeo to understand hazing. It was the hazer's job to keep the steer in line. She opened her mouth to speak, but he held up a hand.

"The drinking got worse after that. I was a quiet drunk. Drank for breakfast, lunch and dinner. Didn't bother anyone. I wasn't the type to fool with women, which is why I've been skeptical about your stepsister's claim that I'm Cole's father."

He paused and looked at her, eyes bleak.

"One particular bender, Lucas called Gramps because he was concerned. Gramps came in the middle of the night and hauled me home." Trevor pulled a chip from his pocket. "Twelve years sober this year."

The chip fairly glowed in the light of the moon.

"That's a huge deal," Hope said softly. She respected him all the more for what he'd been through and the courage he'd mustered to tell her tonight.

"It is." He took a deep breath, as though a huge weight had been lifted. "I like you, Hope. Far more than I expected. I don't know where you and I are going, but I don't want to keep secrets."

"I appreciate that."

"Are you okay with the fact that I'm a recovering alcoholic?"

Hope placed her hand on his. "Trevor, if you're concerned that I'll hold that against you, you're wrong. You're a man of integrity who's been through a lot and turned his life around."

He sighed, releasing a long breath. "Thank you. That's all I expect. An honest answer."

She smiled before another thought occurred. "Cole has been awfully quiet." Hope stood. "I should check on him."

"Mind if I tag along?"

"Sure." She walked quietly down the hall and peeked into Cole's room. He was asleep on the bed with a book in his hand. Patch was at his side. Hope sighed at the tender sight.

The dog looked up, his big brown eyes curious, and he gave a small sound as if asking "what?"

"That's beautiful," Trevor said.

"It is," Hope said. "We have you to thank for it. You've made a difference, Trevor. Don't ever doubt that you're right where the Lord wants you to be."

Hope turned her head, not realizing he was so close. She froze. Unable to move.

For the longest moment, Trevor gazed at her. Then he smiled. "Did you say there was chocolate cake?"

Hope smiled back. "Yes. Come on. I'll even put on a pot of coffee."

"Ever try Gramps's coffee?"

"I have. It's the most disgusting thing I've ever tasted in my life."

Trevor laughed. "Yep. That would describe Gus's killer coffee."

Hope entered the kitchen and moved a domed pink glass cake stand from the counter to the kitchen table. "Wait until you see this cake. I think it's the buttermilk that makes a difference."

"Where'd you get that cake stand?"

"At that home goods store inside Liv's restaurant." She lifted the lid, revealing a two-layer cake with swirls of shiny chocolate frosting. "Perfect. Right?"

"Yeah," he said softly. Trevor's blue eyes were tender as he watched her. "Perfect."

Hope nearly swooned at his words. Her face warmed. Oh, this wasn't good at all. She'd been concerned about Cole getting too attached to Trevor. Her heart whispered that she was falling for the man who might be her nephew's father.

Chapter Nine

"This is living," Gramps said with a happy sigh. He leaned back on his chair, his line in the water, and his feet propped up on a cooler filled with Dr Pepper. "Was that the prettiest sunrise you've ever seen, or what?"

"Yep. It was a nice sunrise," Trevor said without looking up. First, he'd stabbed himself with a lure. Now his line was tangled. He'd been working to untangle it for the last forty-five minutes.

"Nice? That was God's handiwork," Gramps said. "There were more colors in the sky than on the paint chips at the hardware store." He huffed. "You kids take it all for granted."

"Gramps, I roll out of bed at four every morning. I like a sunrise as much as the next guy. But we've been sitting here for four hours now without a nibble. I'll take cattle over fish every day."

Trevor shook his head. Nope, fishing was not his favorite sport. He wasn't even sure it was a sport. Crawling out of a perfectly comfortable bed at dark thirty in the morning to sit on the banks of the Homestead Pass Lake didn't make any sense to him. But he'd do it once a year if it made Gramps happy.

"Fishing is all about patience. Patience has never been your strong suit, Trevor. Relax and enjoy God's gifts all around you." Gus swept a hand through the air like a game-show host. "Hear that water lapping against the shore?"

"I do, and it's putting me to sleep."

"Did you notice that red-tailed hawk that soared across the sky?" Gramps shook his head. "I'm counting my blessings because, if it wasn't for Hope, I might not have been in shape to be here today. I'm mighty appreciative."

Trevor glanced around. "Where is Hope, anyhow?"

"She went over to the other side of the lake to visit your brothers' wives. They've got a fancy tent set up. That's another thing," Gramps continued. "What happened to man and the elements?" His eyes rounded with outrage. "And can someone tell me why there's a food truck in the parking lot?"

"Free enterprise, Gramps." Trevor chuckled. This might not be an opportune time to point out that man and the elements probably didn't include the six-pack of Dr Pepper Gramps had on ice in his cooler.

"I'm hungry," Cole announced over the conversation.

"You gotta talk soft, or you'll scare the fish," Gramps said.

"I'm hungry," Cole whispered.

Trevor dug in his pocket and pulled out a bill. "Here you go. Get yourself a hot dog and grab me one too, please."

"Sure. Thanks, Trevor. Will you watch my line?"

"Absolutely." Trevor glanced over at Cole's line, which was not tangled. Not a bit of movement. The water was clear enough to see to the bottom, but the fish had checked out. The number of anglers lining the shore today had probably sent them into hiding. Gramps was responsible for getting the word out about this event. He'd negotiated with the local press in Homestead Pass and Elk City. The derby had sold out, and the place was wall-to-wall anglers. There wasn't an empty spot on the banks of the lake. Gramps was no doubt having regrets.

"Need anything, Gramps?" Cole asked.

"No thank you, son." Gus patted the ice chest at his feet. "Got everything I need right here. Just like the good old days."

This time, Trevor did laugh.

When Cole was out of earshot, his grandfather stole a look around and then gave Trevor a nod. "You talk to Hope?"

"Yeah, Gramps. I did." His line was nearly untangled. Might be ready to cast again before it was time to head home.

"I appreciate that you are a man of few words, but could you be more specific?"

Trevor raised his head and looked at his grandfather. "It went fine."

"Ha." He slapped his leg, a gesture that Cole had picked up. "Told you so."

"Yes, you did. But let's not get all excited about *fine*."

"Well, sure I will. If I waited for *you* to get all excited, I'd be waiting a long time." He released a breath and smiled. "When do I find out if I have a new grandchild or not?"

"The test results?" Trevor glanced around. "We can't talk about that here."

"Answer the question and we won't."

"I don't know. There's a lot I don't know, to tell you the truth. I don't know what will happen if the test is positive. I don't know what will happen if it's negative. Either way, Hope's headed back to Oklahoma City soon."

"I guess you'll have to figure out a way to get her to stay in Homestead Pass and let her think it was her idea."

"Gramps, that's a little devious. Even for you."

"*Devious* is a strong word." He offered a mischievous smile, his blue eyes sparkling. "You're a smart feller. Put that college education to work."

"I am a smart feller. I've convinced her to volunteer at the Kids Day event. She's agreed to take a vacation after you're released by the doctor."

"See, I knew you were smarter than you look."

Trevor rolled his eyes. "Thanks for the vote of confidence."

"Excuse me."

Both Trevor and Gus turned to see a pleasant middle-aged woman standing near their gear. She held a can of soda in her hand and peered down at Trevor. "Is that your son over there wearing that straw cowboy hat?"

Trevor's gaze went from the woman to Cole, who did indeed have his hat on, along with a striped tank top and cut-off jeans. Despite Hope's encouragement to wear shoes, he was barefoot.

"Yes, ma'am. That's him. Is there a problem?"

"Quite the opposite. You should be proud. I forgot my wallet, and he paid for my soda. He's a fine boy. I wanted to tell you that. You and your wife did a good job raising him."

"He is a good kid. Thanks for letting me know." He smiled as the woman left.

"Aw, that boy nearly breaks my heart," Gramps said. "You did a good thing taking him under your wing. I wouldn't be unhappy to find out he's your kin."

"That's one thing we both agree on," Trevor said. He

still didn't fully believe Cole was…but part of him wanted it to be true.

Cole returned minutes later and handed Trevor a hot dog. "Where's yours?" he asked.

"Aw, I didn't really need one."

Trevor pulled out another bill. "Go get a hot dog. And, Cole, that was a kind thing you did, buying that woman's drink."

"I remembered that last Sunday, Pastor talked about kindness. He said we aren't supposed to let our left hand know what our right hand is doing."

"You got the gist of it, Cole." Trevor nodded. "But the Lord knows, and I'm sure He's proud of you. I sure am."

A grin lit up his face as he raced back to the beverage tent.

"What was that all about?" Hope asked as she approached, her gaze following Cole.

"Nothing," Trevor said. "Just your nephew being a great kid."

"He is, isn't he?" She smiled and sat down on her lawn chair next to her line and adjusted the rod. Trevor had noticed a few anglers stop and chat with her today. He couldn't blame them, though he'd gone out of his way to stand and stretch when they approached.

Just doing his part to keep the yahoos away. He was reminded of Bess's remark that Hope was a little bit of sunshine. Today she wore a yellow tank top and denim shorts with flip-flops. Her hair had been pulled up into a ponytail. A smile was never far from her lips.

Her life hadn't been easy either. It occurred to him that she taught him a lot by example. She'd left home at eighteen. Put herself through college. Gramps was right. Hope kept her eye on the prize. Slow and steady won the race.

"Fish biting on the other side of the lake?" Gramps asked.

"Nothing legal," Hope replied. "Drew and Sam have tossed back half a dozen. Liv and Sadie have pretty much given up. What they do have over there is ham-and-cheese quiche from Liv's restaurant and chocolate croissants." She frowned. "I packed peanut butter and jelly. I'll know better next time."

Next time. Trevor liked the sound of that, and he also liked the silent communication that had developed between them. A single move of her eyebrows or a twist of her lips and he knew exactly what she was thinking. Yep, life was good. Better than he would have expected or deserved.

"Any action on my line while I was gone, Gus?" Hope asked.

"Not even a jiggle. This is getting downright discouraging. Too many people and too much noise, I guess. Those fish are sitting at the bottom of the lake laughing at us."

Hope turned to Trevor. "How are you doing? Anything?"

"One tangled line, a punctured thumb and six mosquito bites." He yawned and checked his watch. "Only four hours until this fun ends. Then I suppose we'll have to stop and get hamburgers for dinner."

"I haven't given up yet," Gramps said. "The day is young."

Trevor groaned and closed his eyes.

"Your arms sure are red," Hope said. "Did you put on sunscreen?"

"Yes, Mom. I did."

"Someone's a little cranky."

He opened one eye and peeked at her. "Yep."

"Aunt Hope, your line is moving." Cole stood behind them, eating a hot dog and pointing at her rod. "Hurry, he's trying to get away."

Hope jumped up, knocking her chair over. "Oh my. You're right, Cole."

"Keep that line tight," Gramps said. He stood and moved closer to Hope. "That's it. Use that drag. Woo-ee, that's a daddy. We won't be putting that fella back."

"He's fighting me," Hope said. "I've never had one this big."

"You want help?" Trevor asked. He stood behind her, trying to get a good look at the catch.

"Yes, please."

Trevor stepped behind Hope and put his hands over hers. "All we have to do is hold on until we tire him out."

Around them, people had moved close to watch the scene, some cheering her on, others filming with their phones.

"Hang in there, Hope," Gramps said. "Trevor is right. No burgers tonight. We might even snag ourselves a trophy."

Hope grinned, her face close to his. "He's slowing down."

"Let's reel him in, nice and easy."

"I got the net," Gramps called, his voice triumphant.

Cole jumped up and down. "You got him, Aunt Hope."

"Here he comes," Trevor said. "Largemouth bass for sure." The fish flew up a bit, splashing water as his tail swished in protest. Gramps netted him and held their prize in the air for all to see.

The crowd that had gathered broke into applause. Hope laughed, her hazel eyes shining. Trevor was certain he hadn't ever seen a prettier sight.

"Let's get him weighed and on ice," Gramps said.

He grinned and shook his head. "I knew it was a good idea to get you on our team."

By noon, Trevor was certain Hope had brought their team to victory, as not a single angler had pulled anything out of the lake that came close to her big boy. He was proved right when the mayor stopped by with a photographer from the *Homestead Pass Daily Journal*. He put a ribbon around Hope's neck and handed Gramps a trophy as the photographer snapped pictures.

"This is the best day I've had since I pulled that home run in the church softball league," Gramps said. He sat in the back seat of the truck staring at the trophy, a silly grin on his face. "They said they'll send us a nameplate with our names on it."

"Can I hold it, Gramps?" Cole asked.

"Of course. It's going home with your aunt."

"Oh no," Hope said. She wiped her face with a towel and fastened her seat belt. "It was providence that fish grabbed my lure instead of yours. They were sitting right next to each other. We're a team. We're the Gus Morgan team. That's what the registration card says. The trophy goes on your mantel, Gus."

"Aww, thanks, Hope."

Minutes later, Trevor pulled the truck in front of the main house, and everyone piled out.

"Whose gonna clean the fish?" Gramps asked.

"Who do you think is going to clean the fish?" Trevor pointed a finger at his grandfather. "Hope caught it. I'm going to fry it up. Cleaning is all yours."

"That's what I was afraid of. You want to put that ice chest on the back porch for me?"

"I can do that," Trevor said.

"Cole and I are going to head home and get cleaned

up ourselves," Hope said. "We'll be back later to help with dinner."

"Sounds like a plan."

Cole grabbed his rod-and-tackle box and started walking down the road toward home. "This was the best fun ever."

"Yeah, it was," Trevor called after him.

"What are you talking about? You complained the whole time," Gramps said.

"Except for getting up way too early and sitting for hours without a nibble, it was fun."

Hope laughed. "That makes no sense whatsoever."

Trevor's gaze skipped over her. Her hair was a mess, tucked up into a ball cap that hadn't kept her nose from turning pink after hours in the sun. The tank top she was wearing had a peanut-butter-and-jelly stain, and her legs were splashed with lake mud. Yep, she was beautiful.

He was certain that he could learn to tolerate fishing if Hope was by his side each time. She made everything more interesting.

Gus released a sigh. "What my grandson is trying to say is that he enjoyed himself in spite of himself."

"Yeah. What Gramps said." It was as though he was waking up from a long sleep. Today he felt more like his old self than he had in a very long time, and he didn't want it to stop.

More and more, he was beginning to think that maybe Gramps was right. He ought to start giving Hope reasons to stay in Homestead Pass.

The afternoon sun warmed Hope's shoulders as she perched on top of the corral fence, waiting for Cole to come out of the stable door. Another first for her nephew. This morning it was fishing. Hope smiled as she thought about the derby. Trevor's hands on hers, his encouragement in her ear as she reeled in the bass. Cole had ended up catching a few as well. Too small to keep; nonetheless, they'd created memories today that would not soon be forgotten.

"What's taking them so long, do you suppose?" Gramps said.

"Trevor said Cole needs to tack up Storm all by himself in order to ride. Those are the rules." She pursed her lips. "You know, Cole hardly touched his fish, and he passed on dessert. I think he's having second thoughts about riding in front of us."

"They better play ball or go home, 'cause I'm about to fall asleep standing up. That fish supper was delicious, especially since you caught it. But it's been a long day and I'm ready for a nap."

The approaching sounds of a horse's hooves and tack jingling had both Hope and Gramps turning toward the stable door.

"Sounds like they're coming," Hope said.

"Oh yeah. There's our boy," Gramps said.

Hope released a small gasp. "Oh, look at him. He looks just like his mother." She couldn't contain her pride. Cole had achieved so many milestones since they'd arrived in Homestead Pass. This might be the most memorable one.

Her nephew seemed smaller and younger astride the Appaloosa. Helmet in place, heels down in the stirrups, Cole sat tall in the saddle with his shoulders back. Tension had his hands a little too tight on the reins, instead of being easy and relaxed, and he didn't look at her or Gramps.

Poor kid was nervous. His gaze remained laser-focused on each step, and he nodded stiffly in response to Trevor's gentle guidance. Trevor continued to reassure Cole while walking next to Storm. The horse and rider moved around the perimeter of the corral in a clock-wise circle.

Come on, Cole. You can do this, buddy.

Hope remembered the first time her father came to watch her ride. She'd been nervous and awkward. Anna, on the other hand, was a natural, confident and relaxed. Her stepsister had been born to ride.

After a few laps around the corral, Trevor led Cole and Storm back toward the stables.

"Way to go!" Gramps hollered. He turned to Hope. "He'll be comfortable in the saddle soon enough. It's wise of Trevor to take things slow."

"I agree," Hope said. There was no rush. Cole had to learn to trust the horse and himself, which might take some time. Trust was the first thing someone lost when adults didn't keep their promises. When that happened, a child learned to be wary and to closely control the few things that they did have control over.

Poor Cole. She'd been there. It was the reason she didn't like to depend on anyone but herself.

"I'm heading back to the house," Gramps said. "They'll be a while."

"Need any help?" Hope asked.

"Naw, I'm good. Tired and old but good."

Hope jumped down from the fence, kicking up a small cloud of red dirt, then started toward the stables to watch Cole groom his horse. Trevor met her at the entrance. He grimaced.

"That didn't go as planned. We even practiced a few fancy steps," he said. "The horse was willing, but Cole was nervous. I couldn't get him to relax. It was like his first time on the horse."

Trevor shook his head. "He's come a long way. I know he talks a good one about the horses, but it's been slow going, building his confidence." He shrugged.

Hope put her hand on Trevor's arm. "You don't need to convince me. I know Cole. Anna has dragged him all over the country. He's been in and out of a dozen different schools. That contributes to his shyness and lack of confidence."

She smiled up at him. "But my heart nearly exploded seeing him on that horse. It's a huge step, and you made it happen."

At that moment, Cole burst out of the stables. He adjusted the red bandanna around his neck and raced up to Hope. "Did you see me, Aunt Hope? Did you see me?"

"Cole, you were like a professional cowboy on that horse," she said. "I'm so proud of you."

"I looked just like Trevor, didn't I?" He searched her face for confirmation that he was just like his hero.

Hope's heart lurched at the words, and she quickly looked at Trevor and then away before nodding.

She sent up a silent prayer. *Lord, whatever happens, don't let this little boy's heart be broken.*

As the new week began, Cole's words continued to play over and over in her head, haunting her waking hours and keeping her up at night. Everything rested on the results of the DNA test, and she wasn't prepared for either result. Once again, she found herself wondering how she'd gone from having a tight lid on her life to it becoming out of control.

On Monday, she and Gus headed to Elk City for his

doctor's appointment, and Hope continued to mull that thought.

"Are you absolutely sure you don't want to let me drive home?" Gus said. "You heard that doctor. I've been cleared. I feel like I should celebrate."

"Congratulations. You put in the work, Gus. I'm proud of you." She signaled and pulled into traffic. "How about an extra Dr Pepper today instead of driving my car?"

Gus frowned. "Is that a bribe from a medical professional?"

"Why, yes, it is."

He screwed up his face in disgust. "I guess we know who doesn't trust me with her vehicle."

Hope chuckled, momentarily distracted from her thoughts.

"Used to be an old-fashioned soda shop on that corner," Gus said as they headed down Route 66. "Trevor's daddy would fit the boys into the pickup and take them for a drive to Elk City. Then he'd take them bowling for the afternoon. It was his way of giving his wife a break."

"That's a wonderful memory," Hope said.

"Yep. Lots of good memories. Do you have some tucked away?"

"My mother… She made me believe I could do anything. When she died, and I was pretty much on my own, it was those lessons she taught me that helped me make it through." Hope sighed, remembering those good times.

"You've been sighing an awful lot today. Everything okay?" Gramps asked.

"Oh, sure—I just have a lot on my mind." She gripped the steering wheel tightly. That was an understatement.

"Something to do with that paternity test?"

Hope hit the brakes and nearly swerved. "What?"

Gus jerked forward and braced a hand on the dash. "Woo-ee. Opening my mouth may have been ill-timed."

"Sorry, Gus. Maybe you could drop further bomb-shells when the car is parked."

"Yeah, I will surely remember that." He released a breath for dramatic effect. "My life flashed before my eyes, and I realized I forgot to make my bed this morning."

Hope shot him a glance. "I wouldn't qualify that as a near-death experience. Trevor, on the other hand, may experience one when I get back to the ranch." She shook her head. "He promised not to tell anyone. I can't believe he told you."

"Aw, don't blame Trevor. I pretty much beat it out of him."

Now she had to wonder who else knew. Was everyone whispering behind her and Cole's back? Was all of Homestead Pass laughing at them?

"My lips are zipped," Gus reassured her.

"Thank you, Gus. I appreciate your discretion."

"Happy to keep my mouth from running," he said. "No need to be concerned."

"I am concerned," she said. "Very concerned."

"Are you worried Trevor is Cole's daddy, or are you worried he isn't?"

Hope offered a begrudging smile. "You pretty much nailed it." She slowed for a traffic light, which turned green, and shot him a quick glance. "When I first arrived, I would have said with complete certainty that I had no plan other than finding Cole's father. When I met Trevor and realized how he and Cole hit it off, I realized that I might lose Cole. It was all I could do not to run in the other direction."

She sighed. "Now? Well, now I think my heart might

break if Trevor isn't his father. That boy loves him, and I think Trevor feels the same way."

"Well, sure he does. Trevor has mentored a few boys over the years. Cole is different. I believe Trevor sees himself in that boy."

She swallowed back the emotion threatening to bring her to tears. "Trevor has helped Cole to heal and to grow. It's been a transformation that could only be divinely orchestrated."

"And you might say the same is true of Trevor. Don't you think?"

"Yes. You're right. Trevor is changing."

"I don't see the problem," Gramps said. "Stay. It's clear as the nose on your face that Trevor cares about you as well."

"He hasn't dated in seven years, Gus. I'm not willing to be the rebound girl who helps him get over his first love. That never ends well."

Hope had spent more than a few nights wrestling with the realization that she was falling for Trevor. That didn't mean she was ready to let go of the roadmap she'd carefully drawn for her future.

"Is that what you think?"

"It's classic. I know Trevor is in AA, but has he had any sort of counseling since his wife died?"

"Can't say that he has."

She nodded. "Trevor is finding Trevor again, and that's a wonderful thing. He'll be ready for a relationship eventually. Maybe even soon. But I'm not convinced that he's ready now." Or maybe she wasn't convinced that *she* was ready. She'd learned to keep her heart guarded a long time ago.

"I'd argue with you, except you're giving me a perspective I haven't considered. It's clear you care for

Trevor too, which makes me think that you're a selfless young lady."

Hope grimaced. Gus had it all wrong. She wasn't selfless. More like self*ish*, because so far the only person she'd ever really trusted was herself.

"Don't give me too much credit," she finally said. "If I have any insight at all, I gained it all the hard way."

"Sounds like you graduated from the school of hard knocks too." He cocked his head. "I was at the top of my class."

She smiled. "Oh, Gus. The Morgan men are so blessed to have you as their guardian. I only hope that I can do for Cole what you've done for them."

"Now you're going to make me blush."

She put her hand on his and squeezed. "I mean it."

"I appreciate that. Now let me give you something to chew on, because you don't get to be my age without learning a few things."

"What's that?" Hope asked.

"Don't discount the hand the good Lord plays in our lives. There's a plan bigger than you and Trevor. We make plans, and the Lord laughs and offers a better way. A way we couldn't even see, because sometimes, we can't get out of our own way."

She nodded as he continued.

"You never know." He shrugged. "My advice to you is to stay open to detours. We get so fixed on the map, that we miss what's right in front of us."

Now Hope chuckled. "My life has been nothing but detours. I always get to point B courtesy of point Z. But, yes, I will keep an open mind."

"That's all I ask."

Was Gus right? Was it time to turn it all over to the Lord? The thought of letting go was almost as difficult as the thought of saying goodbye. Once again, she found herself praying.

Lord, please guide me. Because I've got some hard decisions to make.

Chapter Ten

The rumble and clang of a dually and horse trailer approaching the house caught Trevor's attention the following Thursday and he stopped in his tracks. He'd been about to take Cole out in the ute to check the herd when he turned to see who it was.

"Well, what do you know?" Trevor grinned.

"Who is it?" Cole asked absently. He threw a stick, high and far, and Patch chased.

"The long-lost Morgan brother. Mr. Lucas Morgan."

The truck's horn blasted a staccato beat, and his brother stuck his head out of the driver's window, waving his hat. "Woo! Hoo! Good to be home."

Moments later, Lucas parked the dually, jumped out and raced up to Trevor, grabbing him in a bear hug. Trevor had more muscle, but Lucas had the height, and Trevor was unable to wrestle free from the embrace. Luc laughed like a kid, then finally released him.

"Hey, Trev. Looking good," his twin said. "I see you got your summer haircut."

"Yeah, one of us has to maintain some decorum." Trevor reached for his brother's hat, knowing his brother hadn't trimmed his shaggy hair in months. In response, Lucas laughed and stepped just out of reach.

"That would be you," Lucas said. "The lone ranger. Lazy M boss man. My brother."

"Hilarious, as usual," Trevor observed dryly. "Welcome home, prodigal son. How long are you staying?"

"I'm here at your request. Remember?"

Trevor frowned. "Come again?"

"I came to help you with your summer kids thing. It is next weekend, right?"

"Close. Two more weeks."

"Really? Well, I sure got that wrong." He shrugged. "That's okay. Between you and me, I could use a little break from the circuit. Had a bad spill last week. Ended up with a concussion and managed to bang myself up." He rolled up the sleeve of his cotton shirt and held up his right arm, where a row of fresh stitches trailed from his elbow to his wrist. The arm itself showed signs of fading bruises.

Bronc busting was an accident waiting to happen. Yet, Luc hadn't figured that out yet. With each accident, Trevor prayed his brother would get out of the sport that all the Morgan boys had dabbled in.

Trevor eyed his brother. "I assume you had it X-rayed."

"Yeah. Nothing broken but my bank account." Luc grinned. "Don't tell Gramps, would you?"

"You know Gramps. He finds out whether we like it or not."

"Yeah. Just don't give him any hints. I don't want to worry him." Lucas looked around. "Where is our faithful leader?"

"In the house. He'll be glad to see you."

"How's he doing?" Luc's gaze searched Trevor's,

worry evident in his eyes. "I call him whenever I can, but you know Gramps. Cards to his chest."

"He was cleared by the doctor last week."

Luc nodded. "Good. Good. Don't know what I'd do without the old man."

"I hear you," Trevor said.

His brother frowned and looked behind Trevor. "Hi there, little man."

Trevor turned and put a gentle hand on Cole's shoulder and urged him forward. "Cole, this is Lucas. He's my fraternal twin."

Cole's eyes widened and he looked from Trevor to Lucas. "You don't look the same."

"Nope. We don't," Trevor said. "I'm handsome and Lucas isn't."

Cole laughed. "That's not what I meant."

Trevor smiled. "Some twins are identical, and some are not. Lucas and I are in the *not* category. I'll explain how that works when we feed the chickens tomorrow."

"Nice to meet you, Cole," Lucas said. "Is that your dog?"

"Uh-huh." He patted the energic pup on the head. "This is Patch. Trevor gave him to me."

"Did he?" Lucas raised his brows at the words.

At the mention of his name, the dog barked, did a circle dance and sat down.

Lucas laughed. "Whoa. Look at that. What a neat trick."

"I taught him." Cole grinned.

"Very good."

"Cole, would you take a run up to the stables and see if Jim has any chores he needs help with?" Trevor asked.

Cole furrowed his brow. "We're not going to check the herd?"

"We will. As soon as I visit with my brother."

"Yes, sir." Cole nodded. "Come on, Patch. Come on, boy." The dog eagerly raced his master to the stable.

"'Yes, sir,' huh?" Lucas murmured. "When did you start recruiting ranch wranglers from the elementary school? I knew you were short-handed but come on."

"Funny guy. Cole's here for the summer."

Lucas cocked his head. "I sense a story here."

As they spoke, the door to the main house creaked open, and Hope stepped outside. She waved. Trevor waved back but didn't stop her before she got in her car and headed home. He'd introduce her to Lucas. Just not right now.

It occurred to him that he'd never concerned himself with introducing Luc to a woman before. It was a given that young or old, they swooned over his brother.

But this time, it was different. Trevor wanted to keep his friendship with Hope private for a little longer.

"Who's that?" Lucas asked.

"Gramps's nurse. She came on board so he wouldn't have to go to a rehab facility after surgery."

Lucas gave a slow nod of interest. "Doesn't look like any nurse I ever met, and I've seen my share of late."

"Hope has been a huge help to Gramps this summer. Cole is her nephew. They're staying on the ranch for the summer."

"Looks like I missed all the excitement." He looked at Trevor. "So where's she staying?"

"I invited them to stay at my house."

Lucas jerked back at the news. "Are you kidding me? That's a huge step, isn't it?"

Trevor shrugged. "It's been seven years and the house is empty. I'm not sure why everyone thinks it's a big deal."

"Cut it out, Trev. It *is* a big deal. We both know that."

He glanced in the direction of the departing vehicle. "When do I get to meet her?"

"She's in and out at the main house. I'm sure you'll run into her, eventually."

"Eventually, huh?" He paused as if speculating. "I mean, unless you don't want me to say hello to Gramps's nurse."

"Don't be ridiculous."

Lucas assessed him. That was the trouble with being a twin. You couldn't get away with much. It would be nearly impossible to hide how he felt about Hope from his brother for long.

"Where's your partner in crime?" Trevor asked, trying to change the subject.

He was surprised Harper Reilly wasn't here, following him around. Though in truth, while Harper acted like she barely tolerated Lucas—and in return, he treated her like she was one of the boys—Trevor was certain she was secretly in love with his brother.

"Harper? She followed me all the way from Oklahoma City. Turned off at her daddy's ranch."

"How's the champion barrel racer?"

Lucas scoffed with disgust. "That woman bested me at every turn. She came out in the top three at nearly every stop. Harper is good, Trev. Better than good. Which is why she always buys lunch."

"How about you? Did you stay on the leaderboard?"

"I refuse to answer on the grounds that I'll look like a fool."

Trevor clapped his shoulder. "Come on. I'm the last person to give you a hard time. I washed out of rodeo a long time ago."

"All I can admit is that I'm still in one piece, except for the stitches."

"Make any decisions about retirement?"

Luc nodded, looking contemplative. "I've set a deadline. Next summer, I'll be home for good. Maybe." Trevor's heart perked at the thought. He'd love to have his brother home with him.

Lucas took off his hat and then slapped it back on. "What's for dinner, anyhow? I'm starving. Haven't eaten in hours."

"I'm not sure. I'm cooking tonight."

"You?" He grimaced. "Where's Bess?"

"You're way behind on the news. Bess has been gone for a little over a month, visiting her new grandbabies in Texas. She'll be back sometime tomorrow."

"Texas." Luc raised both palms. "My favorite woman left us for Texas? What's this world coming to? I'm bereft. I got through the last leg of the drive dreaming about warm cinnamon rolls slathered with cream-cheese icing."

Trevor lowered his voice. "Sam might be able to hook you up. Ask him when no one is listening."

"I'll do that." Luc nodded toward the house. "You going in?"

"I will, shortly. Got a few things to take care of."

"Okay, I'll see you later."

"And, Luc?"

"Yeah?"

"Take a shower before dinner."

Luc laughed. "Good to see you too, Trev."

Trevor smiled. It was good to have Lucas home. Seemed like everything was complete when the whole family was at the Sunday dinner table.

Lucas paused and looked Trevor up and down, his gaze penetrating. "You're different, Trev."

"What?" Trevor frowned. "I'm not different. I'm tired."

"No." Lucas shook his head. "It's something else. What's going on?"

"Nothing. You're dreaming."

"Am I?" Luc narrowed his eyes. "I'll figure it out eventually. Twin mind meld and all."

Trevor mulled his brother's words for a moment. Was he different? Maybe so. A lot had changed since he'd last seen Lucas. The last time all four of them had been together was in the hospital waiting room, praying, while Gramps was under the knife with hip-replacement surgery.

Yeah, that was early June. A lot *had* happened since then.

Trevor ran a hand over his face and looked at Lucas. No denying it. His brother was right—he would figure it out eventually. He'd already let things slip to Gramps and his older brothers.

"Hope is here because she thinks I'm her nephew's father." The words tumbled out, and he stood back and waited for the fireworks.

Lucas opened his mouth and closed it. Then he grinned and reached out to hug Trevor again.

"Nope." Trevor jumped back. "Get away from me. You smell like old socks and burnt coffee."

"I can't believe my little brother is a father." Lucas whooped loudly.

Trevor shook his head. It was a good thing they were outside and no one was in earshot. "I'm not your little brother."

"Two and a half minutes, Trev. That makes me your big brother."

"Whatever." He paused. "I know I'm asking the impossible, but could you keep your mouth shut about this?"

"I suppose I could, except that doesn't sound like any fun. Aren't you excited?"

"I haven't let myself get excited." Trevor's throat became tight. In that moment, the truth hit. He was going to be devastated if Cole wasn't his son.

"You've got mail."

Hope dropped her coffee mug into the soapy dishwater and turned to see Bess step into the kitchen. She had mail in one hand and the newspaper in the other.

"Oh, thanks," Hope said. "I didn't realize you were back from the post office already."

"You've got certified mail," the housekeeper said. Her voice reflected curiosity. "Trevor got one too. I signed for them."

"Thanks, Bess." Hope wiped her hands on a towel and reached for the official-looking envelope. She examined the outside, her heart catching at the return address. DNA testing results.

A shiver raced over her. This was it. She'd waited weeks to find out what Cole's future held. What *her* future held. Now that the answer was in her hand, Hope was hesitant to open the envelope.

Thankfully, Cole was gone for the day. Drew and Sadie took him to Elk City to the farmer's market, along with Mae, while Liv babysat little Andrew. It was a nice treat for Cole, and she was appreciative of how the Morgans went out of their way to include him.

"Bess, I'm going to head home. Now that you're back, there's not much for me to do around here."

"You're like me," Bess said. "You have a hard time sitting still. Thanks for weeding my garden this morning."

"I was happy to."

"Trevor says you're on vacation. That means you're not supposed to find anything to do except relax. Go read a book or something."

"Maybe I will." She looked at Bess. "It's really great to have you back."

The older woman offered a kind smile. "Great to be back. I don't mind telling you, I was a little nervous about what kind of disaster the boys might have left me. Wasn't I pleasantly surprised to discover that this place is cleaner than when I left? You might put me out of a job."

"Never. You don't replace family. The Morgans have made it clear that you're one of them."

"Aw, what a lovely way to put things." She smiled. "By the way, I'm going to need that recipe for your chocolate cookies. White chocolate, is it? All I've heard is how delicious they are. You're giving my cinnamon rolls some competition."

"I'm happy to share. However, your cinnamon rolls remain the blue-ribbon winner around here." Hope tapped the letter against her hand. "I'll head out." She scooped up her car keys from the table and turned.

"Oh, and, Hope. Everyone is coming for dinner on Sunday. A little reunion. I'm cooking. Will you and Cole join us?"

"Um, I don't know." Hope hesitated, knowing that the more time she spent with the Morgan family, the more attached to them she became. She glanced at the envelope again, her stomach sinking.

Bess peered at her. "Everything okay, honey? I don't want to be nosy, but is that letter bad news or something? Is there anything I can do?"

"No. No. I'm just tired."

Tired of waiting. Tired of life in limbo. Everything

was out of her control right now and that was the cruelest part of this situation.

Hope drove home slowly, dreading the moment she'd find out what was in the letter. The climb up the stairs to the door seemed the longest of her life. She grabbed a bottle of water, went to the back porch and turned on the ceiling fan before sinking into a rocker.

All the scenarios that kept her awake at night now rolled through her head. Cole was Trevor's son and she'd be forced to leave him behind. Yes, she'd visit him, but that wouldn't be the same. Or there wouldn't be a match and she and Cole would return to Oklahoma City.

Her hands trembled as she turned the paper over. It slipped from her fingers to the wooden planks of the porch floor. She took a calming breath and picked it up.

After slipping her finger beneath the gummed closure, she pulled out the letter.

She skimmed the document, her heart racing. Until she saw the words.

The data does not support a paternity relationship. Probability of paternity is 0%.

The rest of the sentences in the letter became hazy as tears clouded Hope's eyes.

Her breath stuck in her throat and her heart hammered in her chest.

What was she going to tell Cole? *I thought I found your father, but I was wrong?*

Why had Anna put Trevor's name on the birth certificate? Anger at her stepsister bubbled up from deep inside. She closed her eyes tightly as tears slipped down her face.

Hope had so believed that things were going to turn

out all right, which was ridiculous as there was no scenario where the word *right* fit. None.

"Hope? Are you back there?" Trevor called. His voice
traveled from the front yard.

"Yes. The front door is open." She took a breath and
quickly scrubbed the moisture from her face.

"Mind if I come in?"

"Trevor, it's your house." The words came out a little
sharper than she intended.

Minutes later, he stepped onto the porch. His gaze
took in the letter in her hands. Today, his eyes were
bleak with pain. "I'm sorry I'm not Cole's father."

The words nearly gutted her. He was apologizing for
a negative paternity test.

Hope blinked hard. *You will not cry.*

Trevor crouched and took her hands in his. Hope concentrated on the feel of his hands, trying not to think
about the day when he wouldn't be in her life. Trevor was
a good man. He had come alive since Cole entered his
life. Maybe they both had come alive since they'd met
here on the Lazy M.

What would happen now? She couldn't just hang
around because there was a stirring in her heart when
Trevor was near. It was time to move on.

"I care about Cole," Trevor murmured.

"I know you do."

"I care about you as well, Hope."

She took a deep breath. "You're a good friend, Trevor."

"What if I want more than being your friend?" He
searched her face and she had to look away. "Am I imag-
ining that you and I have something?"

He paused. "I know what I want and I'm not afraid
to go after it. What about you? Are you willing to put
aside the fears of the past and go after what you want?"

Then, she dared to meet his eyes. Big mistake. Hope longed to put a hand on his stubbled jaw and tell him how much she cared, but the words were locked inside. Falling for Trevor was a risk. He was right. She was afraid to love him.

"I'm confused, Trevor," she finally said. "I haven't even had time to process that I've spent weeks holding my breath about Cole's heritage only to find out I had it all wrong."

"Are you sorry you came to Homestead Pass?" He searched her face and she looked away.

How could she adequately explain how she felt? The town, the ranch, the Morgans—and yes, Trevor—were all a dream come true. Someone else's dream. This would all be a memory she unwrapped and looked at when she wanted to play what-if someday. But it wasn't her reality.

"Wow. I guess I have my answer. I had it all wrong too, didn't I?" Trevor stood. "What are you going to do?"

"Nothing has changed. I'll be here for your event. I'm looking forward to it." She worked to sound upbeat.

"What about finding out who Cole's father is?" he asked. "That kid deserves so much more. If I was smarter, I would have refused the test and simply claimed him as my own when he showed up. This way hurts. It hurts like I haven't hurt in a long time."

Hope winced at his words. Words that reflected her pain as well. She thought she was following a prayerful nudge to Homestead Pass. Instead, she'd found heartache for everyone.

"Anna never mentioned anyone else," she finally said. "I talked to Cole and asked him if his mom ever discussed a boyfriend, and he said no. I can't go randomly swabbing cheeks of every guy on the rodeo." Again, she tried to make light of things. "I need to get Cole enrolled in school and get back to my life."

"Don't discount this as your life. Your future," Trevor said.

"What does that mean?"

"I spoke to Colin Reilly the other day."

She looked at him with surprise. "Colin Reilly? What does he have to do with anything?"

"Remember that comment he made about wanting to talk business with you?"

"At the barn dance?"

"Yeah. I ran into him in town Wednesday morning."

Tension unfurled in her stomach. "You talked to Colin Reilly about me when I wasn't present?"

"It was casual. I wasn't going behind your back."

"Trevor, the fact that I wasn't there, and I didn't give you permission to discuss me, is going behind my back." Now she was becoming cranky. "You did it when you shared about Cole to your grandfather as well."

Trevor ducked his head and then looked up with a grimace. "Yeah. Maybe this is the time to fess up. I told all of my family about Cole."

Hope gasped. "But we had an agreement."

"I apologize. It was an agreement I should have never agreed to. My family is everything and I found out the hard way that secrets don't work."

"And Colin Reilly?" she prompted.

"He's going to bring his mother-in-law to his home and needs someone he can trust to manage around-the-clock care. I told him what you'd done for Gramps. He was impressed and even mentioned salary and benefits." Trevor rattled on with numbers and specifics.

The more he spoke, the more upset Hope became.

"What do you think?" he asked.

"What I think is that you should have given him my phone number. You were way over the line." She shook her head, unable to believe what she'd heard.

Trevor leaned closer. "No. That's not it at all. This just sort of happened."

"Trevor, I don't need my life managed. I've taken care of myself since I left home. Before that, really. Up until I came here, I've been doing a pretty good job too."

He stood and paced back and forth, his boots echoing on the wood planks of the porch. "We're friends, Hope. More than that, really, and my intentions were all directed at helping you and Cole."

His gaze searched hers then fixed on her hands, held tightly in her lap. "Honestly, Trevor, I don't know what I want anymore."

"Maybe you could let me know when you do. I've made it clear I care about you and Cole. The truth is, I'm in love with you, Hope."

Hope swallowed at the admission. Fear clutching at her heart.

"You're determined not to need anyone," he said with a deep sigh. "I'm guessing I need to wake up and realize that we're not walking toward the same tomorrow."

She shook her head and searched for an answer. Except she didn't have one. Maybe that was the most telling thing. Cole would be more than happy to stay here, and he'd thrive. Somehow, she'd managed to connect her nephew with the man most likely to provide him with everything he needed.

What about her?

Trevor needed to hear that she was okay with an

uncertain future here. Except she couldn't commit to a future in Homestead Pass if it meant giving up the security of life in Oklahoma City.

Needing someone was a risk she couldn't—wouldn't—take.

Chapter Eleven

"This is so cool." Cole stared at the school bus unloading children for Kids Day.

Children ranging in age from six to twelve bounded from the bus and were led to the welcome tent by a volunteer. Trevor smiled, his heart warm with satisfaction as he glanced around the grounds, where white tents dotted the landscape. Kids Day banners in bright colors had been stretched between tents. Overhead, a blue sky confirmed the perfect weather he'd prayed for.

Trevor had prepared for this day for an entire year. Things were getting off to a good start.

"Where did all these kids come from?" Cole asked.

"They're city kids who have never been to a ranch," Trevor said. "Pastor McGuinness coordinates with city churches and I rent the buses."

"These kids are like me before Aunt Hope brought me here," Cole said.

"That's right." Trevor's heart stuttered at the mention of Cole's aunt. Too many long days and nights had passed since the DNA test results arrived, throwing his life into chaos.

Opening that envelope and seeing the results had

been a punch in the gut. Seeing the real panic in Hope's eyes that day had shaken him to his boots.

Hope had managed to dodge him nicely since then. She'd politely declined dinner with the family and kept a low profile at his cottage. When he'd questioned Cole about his aunt, he only said that she was baking. A lot.

Gramps had nagged him at every turn about the situation, while Lucas accused him of trying to keep him from meeting Hope. Sam and Drew at least had the good grace to stay out of his business. Though on more than one occasion he'd caught his brothers giving him the side-eye and talking quietly. Bess kept silent about Hope's absence at the main house as well, the only commentary a clucking *tsk-tsk* when she didn't realize that he was within earshot.

Didn't matter. The situation was out of his hands. He couldn't make Hope care enough to stay.

"What am I supposed to do today, Trevor?"

Trevor looked down at Cole, who wore a pint-size shirt that matched his own. A yellow T-shirt with the Lazy M Ranch logo on the back and the word *staff* on the front. The sight made him smile. He was so proud of how far this boy had come. As proud as if Cole was his own son. The thought only stabbed at his already tender emotions.

"You and Jim are my security team," Trevor said. "Stick with him and keep an eye out for any problems. Call me immediately if you see something that needs my attention."

"Yes, sir. Should I go find him?"

"He's in my office getting batteries for one of the walkie-talkies. But, yeah."

Cole turned and then looked up at him. "Mr. Trevor, can I ask you something?"

"Of course, Cole."

"Why do we have to leave the ranch?" He kicked the dirt. "Don't you want us here anymore?"

Trevor released a breath. The topic most likely to make him grumpy. "Have you talked to your aunt about it?"

"Yes, sir. She says my home is with her now and that's in Oklahoma City."

"Why do you think I don't want you here?"

"Can't think of another reason why we're leaving. Aunt Hope is happy here. I figured you said it was time for us to go." He made a sour face. "Patch won't like that. You know he won't. He'll miss Cooper. Cooper is like his brother."

Trevor nodded. The despair in Cole's eyes was shredding him.

"Who will give Storm apples if I leave?" Cole asked quietly. His quivering voice begged Trevor to throw him a lifeline. "Maybe my aunt is mixed up. Can you talk to her?"

"Sure," Trevor said quietly. What else could he say? The kid's heart was breaking, and with each plea, his was as well.

The boy shot him a grateful glance. "Thanks, Mr. Trevor. You'll have the right words to make her understand we gotta stay."

Trevor nodded absently, though he knew for a fact that he didn't have a single word that could fix things. For the kid's sake, he'd take one more shot even though he'd probably fall on his face again. How could he convince a woman who'd done everything by herself all her life to let him in?

He didn't know.

"I hope so, buddy," Trevor finally said. He glanced at

his phone. Time to do another check of all the activity stations. "Okay, Cole. Remember, you're staff today." He pointed a thumb toward the stables. "I'll check in with you later."

"Yes, sir."

Trevor started toward the corral, where Drew and Sadie were assisting, offering miniature pony rides to eager children.

Both Drew and Sadie waved at him, and he returned the gesture. "Helmet on?" Sadie called to the next child in line.

Trevor moseyed up to the fence to watch, pulling his hat down to protect himself from the morning sun. He'd applied sunscreen. Even that simple act reminded him of Hope.

A moment later, his grandfather joined him, resting his arms on the top rail.

"You continue to amaze me, son."

"Are you complimenting me or insulting me?" Trevor asked. He wasn't in the mood for whatever lesson Gramps was about to teach.

"Both, of course. This event is nothing short of amazing. I'm thinking next year we oughta bring in the press."

"No way, Gramps. It's supposed to be a homegrown event. I don't need press. The only people I want to impress are the kids. That's already been checked off my list." He kept his eye on the corral while he spoke. "We've got six or seven kids at each activity, with two volunteers. Every child gets the attention they deserve. It also ensures that no one gets lost or hurt."

"Fine by me, but I'm thinking you could get a sponsorship and expand. Bring in a few rodeo stars. Sell merch and such."

"Hard pass." He eyed his grandfather. "I appreciate

the input. All excellent ideas, but not for the vision I have for this program."

Gramps nodded. "I respect your right to be wrong."

Trevor laughed.

"Remind me what your vision is for Hope Burke and her nephew."

Zing! There it was. Gramps never missed an opportunity to nudge him in the direction he decided was the right one.

"Gramps, Hope and Cole are in God's hands. I've done all I can do about the situation."

"I don't believe that for a minute."

The squawking static of his walkie-talkie sounded, interrupting the conversation with perfect timing. "Got to go. There's a problem at the medical tent."

Anxiety chased Trevor as he double-timed it over to the tent Hope was monitoring. Last year, there'd been only one incident—barely an incident at all. A sliver from the corral fence.

Trevor dodged kids and prayed that whatever it was this time would be benign.

He stepped into the tent to find Lucas seated in a chair with his arm on an exam table. His cowboy hat rested on the back of his head and the expression on his face said he was enjoying himself. Hope's head was bowed near his as she concentrated on her ministrations.

Lucas said something and she smiled, looking amused and relaxed. Trevor's gut ached, remembering a time when she'd looked at him like that. After a moment, Lucas saw him in the entrance.

"Hey, Trev. I finally got to meet Hope. I guess you forgot to tell me she's as pretty as she is nice."

He didn't forget anything. Trevor's gaze went to Hope. She looked much the same as the first time he'd met her. Pink scrubs, hair in a ponytail and a pink stethoscope around her neck. He grimaced, recalling how he'd messed up both then and now.

"What's going on?" Trevor asked.

She looked at him, then looked away. "Your brother prematurely lost a few of his stitches. There was a small amount of bleeding, which had a few of the children concerned."

"Not my fault. I promise," Lucas said. "One of the kids decided to climb up on the tractor. I grabbed him before he nose-dived and ended up running my arm into the machine. Totally not my fault."

"Sounds serious. I think you should go ahead and remove his frontal lobe," Trevor said. "I'm happy to sign the surgical consent."

"What?" Hope stared at him for a moment and then started laughing.

Her smile was a punch in the gut. He missed her.

"No surgery is necessary," she said. "I'll clean the area and apply sterile strips. He should check in with a physician on Monday."

Trevor nodded. It was good to see Hope smile in his direction.

When he moved closer to check out his brother's arm, the sweet vanilla scent of her shampoo teased him.

"Am I done, Doc?" Lucas asked.

"Nurse Burke," Hope corrected. She pulled off her gloves. "You are officially discharged. Try to be careful when you're jumping off tractors."

"I'll do that," Lucas said.

Trevor nodded to Hope. "Thanks for taking care of him."

"That's my job," she said.

He turned to Lucas. "Come on. I have it on good authority that the snack tent is open. Let's get something to eat."

Minutes later, he and Lucas straddled a picnic table bench in the snack tent with half a dozen empty juice boxes and a bowl of circus crackers in front of them.

"Need anything else, boys?" Bess asked.

"No, ma'am," Trevor said. "This is great. Just like when we were kids."

Lucas popped an animal cracker into his mouth while closely watching Trevor. Then he shook his head.

"What?" Trevor asked.

"I'm your brother. You're supposed to tell me when you fall in love." He gave a shrug of his shoulders. "Though I have to say, you did a good job without me. Hope is sweet and kind and funny. I like her. I wouldn't object to her as a sister-in-law."

Trevor frantically scanned the room, then leaned across the table. "What are you talking about? And whatever it is, could you do it a little more quietly?"

"Got it bad too, huh?" Lucas sucked on his straw, making loud noises until Bess came by and snatched the box from his hand.

"I don't know where you got that random idea but keep it to yourself. Would you?" Trevor dipped his head and stared at the plastic tablecloth. He'd barely admitted to himself how he felt about Hope; he didn't need Lucas making an announcement.

"Do you need a character witness? Is that it? You're kind of a sketchy character."

Trevor gave a short bitter laugh. "Funny you should say that. I actually did two months ago when I was trying to get her to stay at the ranch for the summer."

"Summer is almost over," Lucas said. "She's been here all this time. That's got to mean something."

"She's leaving next week." Trevor stared ahead, seeing nothing except the image of Hope's car driving away.

"What do you want me to do? Borrow her car keys, maybe? Or I could have Sheriff Steve arrest her for first-degree heartbreak." He shoved a handful of crackers into his mouth.

"You're real funny, Luc."

"It's all I've got." His brother shrugged. "Love is not in my repertoire. My theory is that if you don't fall in love, you can't get your heart broken."

"That advice would have had standing in June." Trevor ran a hand over his face and sighed. "Today? Not so much."

"What are you going to do, Trev?" Luc looked at him, compassion in his eyes.

"I don't have a clue, and I'm running out of time and ideas."

"When in doubt, pray." His brother reached into the bowl and chased the last cracker. "And ask for more crackers."

"As usual, you're a font of wisdom."

"You want wisdom, you go to Gramps. Everyone knows that."

Trevor scoffed. "Gramps is the last person I should talk to."

"Drew and Sam bit the bullet and took Gramps's advice and look where they are. Smiling and at peace."

"I'm not desperate," Trevor said. "Yet."

"Look, Aunt Hope. That sign. Do you see it?"

Hope slowed the car and read the banner stretched across the Homestead Elementary School playground fence. "School enrollment."

"Uh-huh. It says all grades. Can we go check it out?"

"It's Sunday. School isn't open on Sunday."

"It will be open tomorrow." His blue eyes pleaded with her.

"Cole, you're already enrolled in Oklahoma City." She'd done that last week.

Cole crossed his arms and stared out the window. "I don't want to go to school in Oklahoma City. I want to stay in Homestead Pass." The words were spoken without emotion.

He was being unreasonable, and at the same time, Hope admired her nephew. No temper tantrum or acting out. Cole simply made his feelings known. Maybe it would be better if he had a full-blown meltdown. She certainly wanted to.

She'd come to Homestead Pass looking for Cole's father and ended up falling in love with the town, with the Morgans and with Trevor. Such foolishness.

"We don't always get what we want," Hope said quietly as she continued driving. "I know you think that stinks."

"Aunt Hope, I never get what I want."

Oh, what a stab to her heart those words were. Hope swallowed, fighting back tears. No crying. She'd learned when she was ten years old that crying didn't help, so she never cried. Until now. She had shed more tears in the last few weeks than in her entire life.

Tears for all Cole had lost. She'd promised him so much and instead she'd allowed his heart to break a little more.

Hope parked the car in front of the bookstore, got out and waited for Cole. He was being terminally slow. Finally, he reluctantly exited the car.

"What are we doing here?" he asked when he joined her on the sidewalk.

"We're going to buy a thank-you gift and a card for Trevor from you."

Cole perked up at that. "May I pick out the book?"

"The book. The card. Everything." She met his gaze. "Pick out something that will make him smile."

"I can do that." He nodded. "I know what he likes."

"Yes. I figured you were exactly the right person for this job." She motioned up the street.

"I'm going to the coffee shop. I'll be back shortly."

"Okay."

Hope waited until he entered, and the door closed behind him with a final tinkling of the chimes. It was only a short time ago that she'd worried about leaving him in the bookstore.

So much had changed since then. Cole was no longer a little boy. He was a young man. Through the window, she could see Eleanor's wide grin as she welcomed Cole. They spoke and then Eleanor looked out the window and waved at Hope. She returned the greeting and started down the street, grateful that during tourist season all the shops were open on Sundays.

Bright yellow signs posted in the window of several shops caught her attention. She stopped and stared at one. The signs advertised a Labor Day sidewalk sale. Labor Day. And that meant the swift entrance of Thanksgiving and Christmas.

Her chest tightened and she kept walking. The maple trees lining Main Street would change colors as summer transitioned into autumn and then to winter. What was Homestead Pass like at the holidays? She envisioned tiny white lights on the lamp poles with red velvet ribbons. The Lazy M Ranch covered with snow came to mind and she sighed. Liv and Sam's babies would arrive right around the holidays. More grandchildren for Gus to dote upon.

Standing outside the coffee shop, she wiped away the moisture that dampened her eyes, then pulled open the door.

"The usual?"

Hope smiled at the young woman behind the counter. "Yes, please. Iced. And to go."

She returned a few minutes later and handed the covered cup to Hope. "I saw your picture in the paper."

"The paper?" Hope frowned, and then remembered. "Oh, the fishing derby. Yes. Strictly the right place when that big boy was hungry."

The young woman held out her hand. "I'm Britt." She smiled. "I like to meet all my regulars."

"Hope. Hope Burke. Nice to meet you." A regular. Funny how such a little thing could touch the heart. Being known as a regular at a coffee shop in Homestead Pass was the sweetest thing she'd heard in a while. She was going to miss this place.

"You too." Hope sipped the beverage before venturing out into the heat again. She walked beneath the awnings on Main to keep out of the sun, once again window-shopping as she made her way back toward the bookstore.

At the floral shop, she admired the blue distressed cart parked outside the door that held glass pitchers filled with sunflowers. Sunflowers were what Trevor bought her. It wasn't so long ago that they'd had dinner and sat on the back porch under a full moon.

Another memory to tuck away.

"Hey there, Miss Hope," someone called.

She looked across the street and spotted Jim waving at her as he came out of the post office.

"Hi, Jim."

The cowboy smiled. "Haven't seen you around much. Congratulations on that bass. Trevor's got that front-page picture on the wall in his office. But I guess you know that."

"Thank you, Jim."

"See you back at the ranch then."

Hope nodded. Yes, back at the ranch. She was going to miss the ranch most of all.

Chapter Twelve

"Cole, are you ready?"

Hope walked through the house, assessing as she went. She'd worked hard on Sunday and Monday, dusting and cleaning to ensure she left Trevor's house just as she'd found it. The trunk of the car was packed. All she needed was Cole's boxes, then they'd go to the main house and say goodbye to Gramps and Bess. She'd promised Sadie and Liv she'd stop by their houses on her way out as well.

As for Trevor, there really wasn't much more she could say. Cole had given him his gift and the card they'd both signed on Sunday. Seeing him again would be a mistake.

"Cole?" she called again.

She'd heard the back door creak a while ago. Maybe he was outside with Patch. Hope stepped outside and was blasted with the heat. August in Oklahoma had a reputation for excess. The heat index had to be at least ninety, the humidity thick and stifling. She stood at the rail, her gaze scanning the empty yard.

Anxiety niggled as she stepped off the porch, walking farther into the yard and peering through the shade trees. When she walked back into the house and headed down the hall to his room, two boxes of his belongings were stacked in the middle of the room. Everything was as it was last night. A *Space Knight* book was on the bed.

Patch wasn't in his crate. The familiar red leash was missing from the hook on the wall.

A shiver raced up her arms. Something wasn't right.

She grabbed her keys from the counter and raced to her car.

In the short time it took for her to get to the main house, she'd worked herself up into a panic. She parked the vehicle, jumped out and headed to Trevor's office in the stables, taking slow breaths and working to calm herself. Cole had probably walked over to see Trevor and Storm one last time.

She'd promised they would visit. Not an unreasonable request and one she planned to honor.

Her sandals slapped against the floor of the stables as she moved down the center aisle, checking stalls but finding Cole in none of them. She'd passed half a dozen before Trevor's office came into view. He sat at his desk, eyes on a computer screen, a phone in his hand, talking to someone.

His eyes moved from the computer to her, and he frowned, surprise registering on his face. He said something into the phone, put it down and stood, just as she entered the doorway of his office.

"Is Cole here?" she asked.

Trevor frowned. "No. Is there a problem?"

"I can't find him anywhere and Patch is with him."

"He's probably taking him for a walk."

"I checked the yard. They aren't out there. I think he ran away." She let out a deep breath, the realization slamming into her.

"Don't get ahead of yourself. I'm sure he's around here somewhere."

"Trevor, he's not. He said he didn't want to leave and I didn't listen to him." She hadn't heard him at all. No, she was wrapped up in her own pity party.

Hope put her fingers against her lips and tried not to sob. "I'm supposed to take care of Anna's baby. I messed this up so bad."

Before she knew what was happening, Trevor had his arms around her. "It's okay, Hope," he soothed, his voice close to her ear. "We're all doing the best we can and you're doing better than most of us."

She pulled away from his warmth and looked into his eyes. "Where would he go, Trevor?"

"I don't know. Cole turned his phone into me on Sunday. I don't have a way to reach him. He could be anywhere." Trevor paused. "His favorite place on the ranch is the stables. He's not here. I would have seen him."

"The bookstore," Hope said. "It's the only other place I can think of. I'll drive into town."

"We'll go together. You go tell Gramps and Bess to keep an eye out for him. I'm going to have Jim take a ride around the ranch in the ute. I'll meet you at my truck."

"Okay. Okay. Yes." Hope raced out of the stables, her feet kicking gravel as she headed to the main house. She found Gramps in the kitchen making coffee and arguing with Bess.

"If that boy doesn't do something to stop her from leaving, I'm going to do it myself."

Hope cleared her throat as she entered the kitchen.

"I was just talking about you, Hope," Gus said.

"Cole is missing."

"What?" Bess dropped the towel in her hand. "Oh my. What can we do to help?"

"Have you checked the elementary school?" Gus asked.

"The elementary school?" Hope frowned. "What are you talking about?"

"While we were cleaning up after the event on Saturday, Cole asked questions about the elementary school. That got the boys telling stories about their days at that school. He seemed really interested. Said he wanted to go to school there. Trevor gently reminded him that he'd be in Oklahoma City for school."

"Oh, my," Hope murmured.

Sunday he'd commented on the banner on the school fence with details about enrolling. Had he really walked five miles into town to enroll himself in school?

His words came back to her. *Aunt Hope, I never get what I want.*

Cole wanted to stay in Homestead Pass. He was tired of adults who didn't hear him and had decided to take matters into his own hands. She didn't blame him one bit.

"You're right. I know you're right." Hope gave Gus a kiss on the cheek. "Thank you so much."

"We'll be praying," Bess called.

Trevor stood next to his truck when she rushed out of the house. "Gus thinks he's at the elementary school. I think he's right. My guess is that Cole is enrolling himself."

"Get in," Trevor said. "We'll find out."

The drive into town was silent. Hope imagined an eleven-year-old boy and his dog walking this stretch of road to get to Homestead Pass. Would he really walk five miles to town? In this heat?

"Maybe someone gave him a ride," she said aloud.

"Could be. Still, it's only five miles and he's a kid with a dog. I used to walk farther when I was his age."

"Cole's not used to walking five miles and it's so hot."

"You're underestimating him. He's worked all summer at the ranch in the sun. I taught him to hydrate. I think that boy is made of tougher stuff than you realize. He'll be fine."

Silence stretched between them once again.

"Were you going to leave without saying goodbye?" Trevor asked, his hands tightly gripping the steering wheel.

"I hadn't gotten that—that far," she stammered. "I have to return the keys to your house." She stared at his profile and then looked away, clasping her hands in her lap. Why was this so hard? Love wasn't in her long-term plans. Neither was an eleven-year-old boy, her heart whispered.

"Don't you think I deserve more than dropping off keys?" Trevor asked.

"Yes. You do. And, yes, I'm an incredible coward. I don't know what else to tell you."

"At least you're honest," he murmured.

Trevor guided the car down Main Street and made a left on Adams.

"Red shirt?"

"What?" Hope blinked and turned toward him confused.

"Is that Cole over there in the red shirt? There's a maple blocking the view. It's the playground of the elementary school."

Hope looked in the direction he pointed and gasped. It was Cole. He sat on a swing in the playground with Patch at his side, looking sad and alone. Poor kid. She shuddered and caught her breath, offering a silent prayer of thanks.

"Do you want to go and talk to him?" Trevor asked.

"Maybe we could go together." Her heart pounded as she waited for his response.

Trevor's lips slowly moved into a smile. "Yeah. I'd like that."

She jumped out of the truck and waited on the sidewalk for Trevor. He caught up to her and took her hand.

"You're the smartest woman I know, Hope."

"Thank you." She paused. "Why are you telling me this?"

"I want you to do what your heart tells you to do, not what fear is whispering. That's what Cole needs from you."

Hope nodded. He knew her too well.

The gate of the playground creaked as Trevor opened it for Hope and then walked through behind her. Patch's ears perked and he looked up, delighted to see them. When he barked, Cole's head popped up. He got up from the swing.

"Aunt Hope." His gaze went from her to Trevor. "What are you doing here?"

"Cole, you forgot to tell me where you were going. I was worried about you."

"I'm sorry."

"What are you doing here, Cole?" Trevor asked.

The boy shrugged. "I wanted to find out about school here. You know. Just in case."

Hope's heart caught as she imagined this boy of hers bravely walking to town and going into the school, alone.

"What did you find out?" she asked.

"I can't enroll without a parent or guardian."

She nodded. "Good thing I'm here then."

Cole looked at her, hope in his eyes. "Really?"

"Yes." Hope pulled him to her and hugged his slim

frame. He smelled like ranch and dog and maybe cookies too. She met Trevor's gaze over the top of Cole's head, and she offered a smile. To her surprise, he smiled back and nodded.

Then she released Cole, her hands still on his shoulders. "That's not to say that every time you want something you can walk into town without telling me, and I'll give it to you." She raised an eyebrow. "But it turns out I wasn't listening to you like I should have. This town is the best place for you to be right now and I'm sorry I didn't realize that."

She turned to Trevor. "We're going to go enroll in school. Do you want to join us?"

The cowboy grinned. "Wouldn't miss it for the world."

"Thanks, Trevor," she murmured as Cole and Patch bounded ahead of them toward the school.

"I didn't do anything."

"Yes, you did. You were my friend, and you didn't give up on me."

"I can receive that. What's next?"

"I don't know. Why don't you stop by the house tonight and we can talk."

Trevor nodded. "Okay," he said solemnly.

Okay. She could work with *okay*, and maybe between the two of them, they'd figure it all out.

Trevor considered the late-afternoon storm to be a sign. Summer rains cooled the pavement and washed away the dust of life. He stepped over a puddle as he approached Hope's house. When spits of rain started again, he picked up his pace and moved quickly up the porch steps.

"Come on in," Hope called. Someday he'd have to

asked her how she did that. How she knew he was there before he even knocked.

For now, he'd focus on today. Today, she'd enrolled Cole in school in Homestead Pass. That left him breathless with hope that maybe there really was a way to a future together.

"Hi, Trevor," Cole said when he stepped into the house.

"Cole, remember what I told you," Hope called.

"Uh-huh, I remember. The grown-ups are going to talk, so read in my room." He rolled his eyes and giggled, which caused Trevor to laugh.

Hope walked into the room and looked at them. "What's going on?"

Trevor shrugged. "Not a thing." He looked at Cole, who snickered.

"Yeah, right." Hope blew a raspberry. "Come on outside. It's started to rain again and there's a breeze." She grabbed a sweater from the chair and led the way.

The rain fell in a gentle rhythm, its sounds soothing his nerves as he settled on a rocker, which he set in motion with his foot. He prayed his heart wasn't going to be broken tonight.

"Nice weather, isn't it?" Hope said. "Autumn will be here before we know it."

Trevor took a calming breath, inhaling the scent of the rain and the land. "You signed Cole up for school. That means you're staying in Homestead Pass, right?" He looked over at her, seated in the rocker with one leg tucked beneath her and the other on the floor, and sent up a silent prayer.

"I am. I don't understand it, but this is where I'm supposed to be. Of that, I am finally certain."

She rocked back and forth slowly for minutes and

then stopped and looked at him. "You knew all along the results of the DNA test would be negative, didn't you? I mean, you kept hinting at it, but you knew."

He nodded. "I never had that sort of relationship with your stepsister."

"Why didn't you let us just get the tests and be done with it?"

"I told you. I wanted Cole to have time to heal. That was the truth." He raised a shoulder. "Besides, from the minute you stormed onto the scene, I knew there was something about you. If we had a quick test, you'd be gone, and I wouldn't get a chance to figure out why you were the woman who awakened my sleeping heart."

"What are you saying, love at first sight?" She cocked her head. "If anything, it was Cole who stole your heart."

"Nope. You did and I just didn't know it then. Nor did I know what to do about what I felt."

She nodded. "I get that… What I feel for you terrifies me as well."

He looked at her. Hope Burke, so in control, was terrified of her feelings for him. That was a revelation that gave him pause.

"I called Colin Reilly this afternoon. I have a job."

Trevor blinked at the words. She had a job and Cole was enrolled in school. Hope really was staying. He longed to let out a whoop, but he subdued himself, afraid he'd scare her off. "That's great."

"It is." She nodded. "Trevor, you and I know better than most people that every single day is a blessing. I've been cowardly. But I don't want to live life that way anymore."

"So what do we do about it?" he asked.

"The thing is, I'm looking for a forever home, just

like Cole. This town, you, your ranch and your family, are more than I've ever wanted."

"I don't see the problem. Say the word and I'll get the ring."

She smiled. "Two and a half months, Trevor. We've known each other two and a half months. That's the problem."

"My parents knew each other thirty days and they were married twenty-five years, until they died."

"They aren't us." She sighed. "We come with our own baggage. Lots of it."

She was right. Recently, he lived in constant fear that this joy he'd found would be snatched away. "Okay," he said. "What do you propose? Pun intended."

"Cole and I are going to live in Homestead Pass. I'll find a place in town to rent. He can come out to the ranch on Saturdays." He nodded slowly.

"Ask me to marry you in a year. One year from the day we met. One year for you to learn to trust the Lord with your future, and put aside your past, and for me to learn to let go and let God." She looked at him tenderly. "One year to trust the Lord with all of our tomorrows."

His heart swelled as she spoke. He wanted to see her and Cole every day for the next year, until they could be a family. "You have yourself a deal. When do I get to let Cole know that I love his aunt and I'm going to be his father?"

She stood up. "Right now. He's going to be so happy." A smile touched her lips and the hazel eyes glowed with pleasure. "You really love me?"

"I haven't made that clear?" He got up as well. Taking her hands in his, he looked into her eyes. "Hope Burke, I'm in love with you. I'm fairly sure I have been since that day you arrived with your sassy attitude and your pink stethoscope."

She put her arms around his neck. "I fell for you at the same time. After all, how could I resist a man who growled at me?"

"Does that mean you love me back?" His heart thudded in his chest.

"I love you, Trevor. I wasn't looking for love, but it found me."

He touched his forehead to hers, inhaling the sweet scent of her hair. "You know that I'm a recovering alcoholic, Hope. I've made lots of mistakes on top of that."

"No, you're a sinner saved by grace. That's what you told me. Start believing it."

"I'm trying," he breathed. "I'm trying."

She pulled down his head and reached up to touch her lips to his. He returned the favor, kissing her with the intensity of all the love in his heart.

Then, he lifted his head, dazed with the wonder of knowing she loved him.

"Thank you for coming into my life."

"You're the one who called the home health agency. You brought me into your life."

"Gramps is right," he said. "I'm a lot smarter than I look."

Hope laughed and kissed him again. Then she took his hand. "Let's go tell Cole we're going to be a family."

Trevor smiled, knowing all the broken pieces of his heart had come together tonight. *Thank You, Lord. I am blessed.*

Epilogue

One year later...

Hope stood at the front of the church, with Gus Morgan at her side. One year ago, she'd gone looking for her nephew's father. Though she never found him, she found a forever family for her and Cole.

She touched the strand of pearls around her neck. Something borrowed from Liv. The single pearl drops at her ears were new. A gift from Gus. She'd cried when she opened the velvet-lined box.

Tucked inside her bouquet of pink and white roses was a small photo of her mother. Something old. Hope glanced down at her shoes. Baby blue.

Yes, she was more than ready.

Pastor McGuinness cleared his throat. "Dearly beloved, we are gathered together in the presence of God to join together this man and this woman in holy marriage.

"Let us bow our heads in prayer. Dear Lord, we ask You to bless this union between Hope Mary Burke and Trevor Augustus Morgan. Pour out Your abundant blessings in their comings and goings, in joy and in sorrow, and in life and death."

The simple but heartfelt prayer had Hope near tears, her heart bursting with joy.

The congregation that packed the Homestead Pass Church this Saturday morning in August chimed in, "Amen."

Hope blinked back her emotion and snuck a peek at Trevor. His eyes were glassy as they met hers.

Her gaze traveled to the groomsmen—Drew, Sam and Lucas—standing tall, dark and swoony, as Liv had described them a year ago. Directly to Hope's left was her beautiful bridal party. Bess, Liv and Sadie were dressed in soft pink dresses.

"Who gives this woman to be married to this man?"

Gus stepped forward. "I surely do. And it's about time."

A titter of laughter went through the congregation

"Thank you, Gus," Hope whispered.

"You can call me Gramps now," he said.

Hope kissed him gently on his cheek before he sat down. She handed her bouquet to Bess, her matron of honor, before stepping toward her groom.

Trevor took her hands in his, tender emotions shining from his blue eyes. In that moment, Hope knew that she would never love him more. He'd given her so much. A home, a family and his heart. His willingness to wait a year to get married broke down the last remnants of fear stubbornly guarding her own heart. In return, she had given him time to forgive himself and prepare for this new journey.

He claimed that waiting a year had only made his love grow more and more. She agreed. Her heart had expanded as she learned to trust that he'd never let her down.

Patch gave a short, excited bark and danced in a circle. "Sit, Patch," Cole said. Then he stepped back into his position next to Trevor as best man. The dog complied and sat at Cole's feet, the pink ribbon around his neck slightly askew. The obedience lessons with Jim had finally paid off.

Cole, so handsome in his tux, gave her a thumbs-up. Anna would be so proud of her boy. "Thank You, Lord," Hope whispered.

"Please be seated."

It took a few minutes for the congregation to settle. Half of Homestead Pass was in attendance, and Hope wouldn't have it any other way. After the ceremony, they'd head to the Lazy M Ranch, where Liv's aunt had catered the outdoor reception.

As the church became quiet, the sweet babbling of Liv and Sam's twins echoed from the back where they sat with Liv's aunt.

Behind Hope, in the second row, she heard Eleanor Moretti whisper, "You know I got them together. I imagine they're going to name their first child after me."

The ensuing words of love and union were a blur of happiness to Hope's ears. Cole proudly produced the rings and moments later, Pastor McGuinness declared that they were man and wife.

Trevor held her tenderly and pressed a soft kiss to her lips.

"I love you, Hope. Always and forever."

"I love you too, my cranky cowboy."

Hope retrieved her bouquet, and they walked down the aisle accompanied by the cheers of their family, friends and all of Homestead Pass.

As they sat in the limo, courtesy of Colin Reilly, Trevor leaned close and kissed her again. "When we get back from the honeymoon, I want to adopt Cole officially. I want us to be a family."

"Yes," she breathed against his lips.

From the front seat, the driver turned and smiled. "Ready to head to the reception, Mr. and Mrs. Morgan?"

"Yeah, we're ready," Trevor said.

"More than ready," Hope added.

* * * * *

If you enjoyed
The Cowboy's Secret Past

Be sure to check out the other books
in Tina Radcliffe's Lazy M Ranch series.
Available now from Love Inspired!

Discover more at LoveInspired.com

Dear Reader,

Thank you for taking the time to read this installment of the Lazy M Ranch series. With each book, another Morgan brother not only falls in love but also recognizes God's calling on his life.

This book is one of my favorites because of the theme of forgiveness. Like Trevor, all of us fall short. But fortunately, we have a path beyond our shortcomings.

Jesus's death on the cross provided a way for us to have our sins forgiven and unite us again with God. My prayer is that you embrace this act of selfless reconciliation, and the incredible love God has for you and me.

I hope you fell in love with the family that Hope, Trevor, Cole and Patch created. I've included a few of the recipes found in this book on my website, www.tinaradcliffe.com.

Again, thank you for taking this journey with me. The support of readers means so much. I always look forward to your comments on social media and your emails.

Sincerely,
Tina Radcliffe

COMING NEXT MONTH FROM
Love Inspired

AN UNCONVENTIONAL AMISH PAIR
Seven Amish Sisters • by Emma Miller

When her employer's son returns after an eight-year absence, Henrietta Koffman fears she'll lose her handywoman job—but ends up with a helper instead. As they work together, neither can deny the attraction or the underlying problem—Chandler Gingerich isn't Amish. With a little faith, can an unlikely pair become a perfect match?

THE AMISH BAKER'S SECRET COURTSHIP
by Amy Grochowski

Opening a bakery has always been Cassie Weaver's dream—one that hinges on her good friend Martin Beiler. Now Martin's home to fulfill his promise to help set up her bakeshop. But when everyone suspects they're secretly dating, will their pretend courtship begin to feel like more?

BONDING WITH THE BABIES
K-9 Companions • by Deb Kastner

After she rejected his public proposal, Frost Winslow never thought he'd see Zoey Lane again—until she walks back into his life with their twin babies. Now they're learning how to be parents together and starting over. But a real family could be in their future...if Zoey makes peace with her past.

HIS UNEXPECTED GRANDCHILD
by Myra Johnson

Lane Bromley is shocked when he learns he has a grandson. Now he's caring for the little boy—except his paternal grandmother, veterinarian Julia Frasier, thinks the child belongs with *her*. But finding a compromise is one thing. Accidentally finding love is quite another...

THE COWBOY'S RETURN
Shepherd's Creek • by Danica Favorite

Leaving his troubled past behind, Luke Christianson returns to his hometown to care for his grandmother—and discovers he's a father. As he gets to know his teenage daughter, Luke and Maddie Anter, the mother of his child, grow closer. Will a family conflict stand in the way of their happily-ever-after?

A FATHER'S VOW
by Chris Maday Schmidt

Dedicated to protecting his daughter and hometown, widower Constable Jack Wells will do anything to stop the vandalism at their beloved wildlife preserve—even partner with its new veterinarian. Soon their on-duty stakeouts evolve into off-duty family outings. But with heartbreak in their pasts, are they ready to risk a second chance?